VELI UNVEILED

MISSION EIGHT

JOHN P. LOGSDON

CHRISTOPHER P. YOUNG

CRIMSON MYTH
PRESS

Published by: Crimson Myth Press (www.CrimsonMyth.com)

Cover art: Jake T. Logsdon (www.JakeLogsdon.com)

Thanks to our fantastic Reader Team!
(listed in alphabetical order by first name)

Adam "Beefy" Pederick, Alex McKenzie, Allen Maltbie, Amy Simmonds, Andrea Tootell, Andy Crank, Annet Davidson, Aragorn Berner, Arto Suokas, Barrie & Muriel Mee, Benny Bennett, Bob Gouldy, Bob Topping, Brian Floyd, Camille Green, Candy Valdez, Catherine Currie, Cher Eaves, Chastity Jackson, Chris Hargrave, Chris Anthony, Chris Wakeham, Christopher Ridgway, Clare Short, Conrad Z-ro, Darrell Northcott, Dave Watson, David P. Ridgway, Diann Pustay, Earl Brown, Eric Hirsch, Eric Ludwig, Erin Mattox, Fergy Ferg, Geoffrey Ackers, Grant Taff Lewis, Gretchen Wickline Carter, Helen Wrenn, Helena Coker, Holly Roth-Nelson, Hugh Davies, Ian Nick Tarry, Igloo Q. Birdbath, J. Ed Baker, Jack Tufford, James Robinson, Jamie Smith, Jan Gray, Jason Mills, Jenna Burns, Jennie Nichols, Jennifer Willison, James Hannah, Jo Freeman, Jodie Stackowiak, Joe Simon, Joel Jackson, John Barbaretti, John Chappell, John "Yiaagaitia" Debnam, John "Murphyfields" Ladbury, John Scott, John Weaver, Julia Taylor, Keith Hall, Kevan Busby, Kim Phelan, Lee Goodrow, Leigh Evans, Les McCandless, Lesley Donnachie, Leslie Grotti Jost, Linda Carter, Lizzie Fletcher, Madeleine Fenner, Mags Kelly, Mahri McGregor, Mark Brown, Martin Smith, Matthew Wilson, Michael Crosby, Mike Black, Mike Ikirt, Neil Gurling, Neil Lowrie, Nic Jansen, Nick Moon, Nigel Brett, Noah Sturdevant, Paul Deakin, Paul McCarthy, Paul Raymond, Paul Turner-Smithson, Paulette "Elsolel" Kilgore, Phyllis McGrath, Rachel Blakeman, Richard Doubleday, Sammie Elestial, Sandee Lloyd, Scott Ackermann, Sean Ellis, Sharon Ward, Shirley MacDonald, Sion Morris, Stephen A. Smith, Steve

Grossman, Steve Hayes, Steve Shamka, Tammy Wilson-Lewallen, Teresa Cattrall Ferguson, Terry Foster, Thomas Mayes, Tony Dawson, Tony Dodds, Tracey Herron, Traci Hoffman, and Yelaerb-Gnortsmra Hag Erialc.

NEW ORDERS

rexle sat in Lord Overseer Veli's office for the first time since returning from Fantasy Planet.

As always, Veli was playing coy, tapping the desk at regular intervals. Frexle couldn't see the Lord Overseer since he kept himself sequestered in the shadows, but the depth of his voice and the power of those taps made it clear that the man was powerful indeed. It was assumed that if you ever actually saw Lord Overseer Veli it assuredly would be the last thing you ever saw.

But Frexle didn't feel like his normal pensive self. He had just found new information about the Lord Overseer that was interesting. Very interesting.

Frexle was damn certain that Veli was the owner and creator of Fantasy Planet. He hadn't shared this information with anyone else, of course, but were he correct the proverbial zebble—which is a cat-like creature from Frexle's homeworld of Zibble—would be let out of the bag. Not that they kept zebble's in bags on Zibble or anything. It was just a saying.

For most people it wouldn't matter if external interests

were maintained, but there was a strong rule that government officials were disallowed from doing business until they left power.

Frexle had wanted to start up a yogurt shop in the Oobow district, for example, but Veli threatened to shred the skin from his person if he even toyed with creating a business plan. It was even rumored that a few senators had been assassinated because their secret investments in various firms had been discovered.

So if Veli *was* involved with this Fantasy Planet, it would be quite a nugget of information.

"I have a very important mission for your beloved Platoon F, Frexle," Veli said in his gravelly voice.

"Oh?"

The tapping stopped.

"Don't you mean, 'Oh, my lord?'"

"Sorry," Frexle said, not really feeling sorry. "That's what I meant."

"Don't you mean, 'Sorry, that's what I meant, my lord?'"

"Yes."

"Don't you mean …" Veli trailed off and growled lightly. "Nevermind. Anyway, a new upstart planet called Lopsided-11 is gaining a fleet of technologically-advanced ships and they must be stopped."

One of the primary tenants of the Overseer government was to ensure that no universal body could grow to the point of usurping them. To this end, Lord Overseer Veli created a program that constantly scanned the cosmos in search of planets that contained life. The celestial bodies were then surveyed, studied, and placed into an algorithmic matrix that determined their propensity to compete with the Overseers. If a threat was uncovered, whether that threat be immediate or predicted to be a concern 10,000 years into the future, the planet was flagged. Once flagged, the planet was slated for destruction.

Well, historically anyway.

Ever since Frexle had found *The SSMC Reluctant*, and since the *HadItWithTheKillings* group started gaining influence, the Platoon F crew had been used to dissuade cultures from continuing down their technological paths in order to avoid extinction. So far it had worked perfectly.

"Lopsided-11?" Frexle said finally. "I've never heard of this planet … um, my lord."

"Not surprising," replied Veli. "There are billions of planets out there, you know."

Frexle brought up his datapad. "True, but Lopsided-11 is not listed anywhere in your program as a threat. In fact, it's not even listed at all. What sector is this in?"

Veli banged his desk powerfully.

"Are you doubting me, Frexle?"

"I'm just trying to understand, sir," Frexle said, feeling a rush of adrenaline.

"You don't need to understand, Frexle. You must merely do as you are commanded."

"Yes, sir," Frexle said. He was aggravated that his normal reaction to Veli's outbursts was fear. The Lord Overseer *could* undoubtedly snap Frexle in two in the blink of an eye, or at least that was what everyone believed. He cleared his throat and added, "Has the senate been informed …"

"I do not require the permission of the senate for trivial things," Veli said, cutting Frexle off. "They are already aware of the fact that Platoon F was brought on board for this purpose. We don't need a vote every time some half-baked planet begins growing too quickly."

"Hmmm."

The tapping had stopped again and the room fell silent. It also seemed to get about ten degrees colder, as if someone had opened a window in the middle of a blizzard. Frexle fought to avoid shivering, but it wasn't easy.

"You're acting strangely, Frexle," Veli said accusingly.

"I am?" Frexle squeaked.

"I've noticed your attitude growing ever since we brought this Platoon F crew of yours on board. This *HadItWithTheKillings* group has been gaining power, too, and that's another thing that appears to be leading to your new-found confidence."

"Well …"

"And I don't like it."

"Sorry."

"Don't you mean, 'Sorry, my lord?'"

Frexle didn't reply. He knew that his lack of response could well mean the end of his existence, but the little fire inside of him was burning brighter than normal. He remembered the words of *Woof*, his favorite character from the TV show *Stellar Hike: The New Crew Aboard*. The Klungin had said, "It is a good day to die." Frexle didn't actually feel that way. He much preferred to live. But it was better to die at the alter of his scruples than to live in a chattering mass of terror.

The tapping resumed.

"I suggest that you get your head back in order before I have you replaced, Frexle. You *do* know what being replaced entails, yes?"

"Yes, my lord."

"It means you'll be killed."

"I know, my lord."

"Kaput. Squashed. Lifeless. Dead. No more. Pushing up the daisies. Worm food. Climbing the—"

"I get it, my lord," Frexle snapped. Then he drew in a quick breath, realizing that he'd leaped rather far over the line.

4

Veli growled and his desk pushed out a little. Frexle still couldn't see the Lord Overseer as the shadow ran too deep, but there was little doubt that the man was standing, ready to pounce. Frexle swallowed hard as his life flashed before him.

But Veli didn't attack.

The desk pulled back more deeply into the shadows and Veli's chair whined slightly, signaling Frexle that the Lord Overseer had sat back down.

"Something is different about you as of late, Frexle, and it disturbs me." The way it was said wasn't laced with angst. If anything, it sounded pouty. "It's like my threats no longer hold any weight over you."

"Should they?" Frexle ventured, hoping that his superior would take this as a chance to grow as a leader.

"Well, of course! How can a manager be effective without the ability to incite fear, chaos, confusion, and concern in his underlings?"

"Motivation maybe?" Frexle suggested. "Or possibly a genuine caring for the well-being of the workers?"

Veli burst out in a fit of laughter. Obviously, Frexle's hope that Veli could ever grow into anything more than a dictator was naive.

"Good one, Frexle," Veli said, after a few moments. "If nothing else, you *are* humorous."

"Thanks, my lord."

"Seriously, though, you've been changing a lot, and ever since you've returned from Fantasy Planet it's gotten really noticeable. Something happened there, I'm sure of it."

"Yes," Frexle said with a slow nod. "Something indeed did."

"Hmmm." Veli tapped again for a few moments. "The way you were talking about the person who had developed the software for that planet when you had given me your mission debriefing was pretty disparaging. Maybe this has something to do with it?"

"Likely."

"But why?"

"Because the programmer had been an imbecile," Frexle stated firmly, recognizing that the end was probably near for him anyway. "To see someone create something so popular that has very little substance is an affront to the cosmic intellect. It's akin to one of those Yogsdon and Lung novels."

"First off," Veli argued icily, "Yogsdon and Lung happen to be my favorite authors …"

"Not surprising."

"… and secondly, I would imagine that the Fantasy Planet creator would far surpass *your* capabilities in *any* field."

Frexle crossed his legs and squinted into the darkness.

"May I ask why you are so defensive of the builder of that planet, my lord? Do you know who it is, maybe?"

"Uh … no. It's just that you shouldn't be such a weenie, Frexle. I mean, creating something like that is highly complex."

"Fair enough," Frexle said with a nod. "It *is* impressive. But there were so many mishaps in the brief snippets of code that I was able to get a look at. It made me sad for the feeble-minded fool. Amateurish stuff, you know?"

Veli growled and the desk rumbled.

"The lack of comments demonstrated that the developer was too sure of his, or her, capabilities, which wasn't warranted in the slightest."

The growling grew louder.

Frexle began to sweat, but he couldn't stop himself. If these were his final minutes, he was going to go out with a clear conscience.

"And the use of antiquated procedural programming methodology over the object-oriented scheme in use today clearly denotes that the responsible party is rather old-school indeed."

"Object-oriented programming wasn't taught when ..." Veli coughed. "Forget it. I have had about enough of this." The tapping continued in triple-hits now, as if the Overseer were thinking about something. "Actually, you have given me an idea, Frexle."

"Is that so?"

"Yes. I've decided that you will go along with the Platoon F crew on this mission."

"What? Why?"

"Because," Veli said at length, "I think that would be wise. You need a new perspective. Maybe I will even have you report to this Captain Harr fellow for the duration of the mission."

Frexle sat straight up. "That would be undignified!"

"Exactly."

"But—"

"Of course, if you would prefer the alternative, I can arrange to find your replacement."

To be put on the *Reluctant* as a subordinate was tantamount to being told to pick up a shovel and start digging one's own grave. Well, maybe not *that* bad, but it was going to be humiliating.

Live to fight another day, he told himself.

"Fine," Frexle replied with a sigh.

"Fine, what?"

Frexle closed his eyes and drew in a deep breath. "Fine, my lord."

"There," Veli said with a chuckle. "That wasn't so bad, was it?"

"No."

"No, what?"

NEW TO THE CREW

Captain Don Harr was staring up from the Captain's Chair. He'd seen a lot of strange circumstances over his years, but this seemed particularly wrong. It was clear that the rest of his crew felt the same way, too, as they were all staring at the same thing.

That thing was Frexle.

"And he wants you to report to me?" Harr asked with a squint.

"That's correct, Captain," Frexle replied stoically.

"Haha," Ensign Brand Jezden said in his surfer-way. "What a douche."

Frexle frowned. "Excuse me?"

"That Veli dude, I mean. Sounds like a real knob."

"Ah," Frexle said, relaxing slightly. "Yes, that he is. I think."

Harr pushed up from the chair and walked around the bridge. He kept his hands clasped behind his back as he looked from station to station.

Ensign Brand Jezden had his feet up on the console. Kicking back and acting like an arrogant tool was his modus operandi.

Lieutenant Hank Moon was at the helm. He was a beautiful, dark-skinned beauty who was quite voluptuous. Technically, he was a *she*, from an anatomical perspective, but Hank was originally programmed to have multiple personalities. Three of them, to be exact. There was Hank, Laasel, and Gravity. All of these personas had been merged together a number of missions ago, with Hank and Laasel complimenting each other perfectly. Gravity, who was a female stripper, had been thought lost, but she had made somewhat of an appearance during their last mission.

Next up was Lieutenant Brekka Ridly. She was military with an edge, wearing short hair and no makeup. It just wasn't her style to get girly about anything, except Ensign Jezden now and then. She was also one hell of a software engineer who had helped the crew out of a few tight jams over their years together.

The next two stations were taken up by a couple of cavemen—though they preferred the term Early Evolutionary Humanoids—who had been picked up from their prehistoric planet of Mugoog during the last Platoon F mission. Grog was obviously the alpha of the two, usually speaking his mind first, but Vlak wasn't one to mince words either. Together they could be quite trying.

Commander Kip Sandoo was a by-the-book soldier. Tall, broad-shouldered, and straight-up military. Fortunately, Harr had been working tirelessly to rewrite that book over their time together. Still, Sandoo was the first to quote regulations and he was ever loyal to the ship and its crew.

The ship's chief engineer, Geezer, was an old-style robot who sported a block torso, spindly arms with claw-like hands, and antennas that stuck off his noggin. He was also one hell of an inventor, giving *The SSMC Reluctant* countless tools, such as instantaneous travel, time travel, teleportation, and a plethora of other amazing goodies. The robot came from the G.3.3.Z.3.R. line, which was the basis for his name.

And now, thanks to Lord Overseer Veli, there was Harr's former boss: Frexle. He was humanoid with curly brown hair. He looked to be middle-aged and was roughly Harr's height and build, and his green eyes were painted a little too largely on the canvas of his lean face.

Harr looked at Frexle and sighed.

On the one hand, he couldn't help but feel a sense of interest in lording over his previous commanding officer; on the other hand, he'd done that before with Rear Admiral Stanley Parfait back when they were both members of the Segnal Space Marine Corps. It just wasn't in Harr's genetic makeup to be cruel to his subordinates, regardless of how they got there. Besides, Frexle had proved to be a decent boss, as bosses went, and it was clear that Lord Overseer Veli was *not* good at management. On top of that, Harr was no dummy. At some point it could well be that Frexle would return to being in charge of Platoon F.

But Harr just didn't know what to do with him.

"Problem is, Frexle, that I've already got plenty of people on the bridge."

"Well," Frexle said, matter-of-factly, "you'll clearly need to make room for one more."

Harr didn't take too kindly to being spoken to that way from a superior, much less a crewman. "Actually," he said, "I really don't."

"I command that you—"

"Excuse me, sir," Commander Sandoo said, taking a firm step towards Frexle, "but I would ask that you not speak to Captain Harr in that way."

"Now, you listen here—" began Frexle while wagging his finger at Sandoo.

"Frexle, stop," Harr stated, cutting off the Overseer. "I

don't want this to be any more uncomfortable than it has to be. The bottom line is that you've been assigned to report to me. Like it or not, that's the assignment. You've been a decent commanding officer to us, and I shall endeavor to repay that favor, but just as I respected your command, I ask that you now respect mine."

Frexle's shoulders slumped and he slowly nodded.

"You're right," he said like a man who'd just been cowed. "I'm sorry. I'm just not used to this. It's very difficult."

Harr patted the man on the shoulder before sitting back down in the Captain's Chair.

"I know," he said as he casually clicked at a few of the switches on the armrest that no longer worked. "Look, these things happened all the time in the Segnal Space Marine Corps. One day you're the brass and the next you're knocked down a couple of ranks. Or, worse, you're a lowly soldier who gets caught up in a military mistake that lands him as the captain of a starship that's being run by a group of maniacal Overseers." He quickly looked up. "No offense."

"No, no," Frexle replied, nodding his head. "I get it. Frankly, it's becoming tougher and tougher to disagree with your crew's sentiment on that. We do appear to be a bunch of, well …"

"Assholes?" Jezden offered.

"I suppose."

"Again, Frexle," Harr said, taking another glance around, "I just don't have any seats up here to fill."

"Sure there are," Frexle argued. "Just throw one of these people out."

"Bastard," said Grog.

"Tool," agreed Vlak.

"All right, all right," Harr said, waving at them. "Pipe down." He then looked back at Frexle. "I'm sorry, Frexle, but they're right."

"I'm a bastard and a tool?" Frexle said, looking affronted.

"No, I mean that they've all earned their positions on the bridge. You haven't. I'm not going to just throw one of them out because it would be convenient for you."

"Then what am I supposed to do?" Frexle whined.

"I'll have to think about it," Harr replied. "I'm sure we'll find something soon enough."

"I'll take him, honcho," Geezer said.

"Pardon?"

"During our last mission he was pretty decent with engineering," Geezer answered, his eyes dimming. "A little rough around the edges, maybe, but that's easily fixed up. I could use another set of hands for some of the inventions I've got going on and he'd be a decent fit. Besides, I haven't had the chance to boss someone around since before you were born, hotdog."

"Boss me around?" Frexle said with a humph.

"Well," said Harr, "that's settled then."

Frexle looked shocked. "It is?"

"Yes. Now, what are our orders from Veli?"

"Says here, thir," said Lieutenant Moon, "that we're supposed to go to a planet called Lopthided-11 and stop their advancement."

"What do they have going for them? Warp drives? Time travel? Discovery of Fire?"

"Still making fun of that, Captain?" said Grog.

"It was a big deal to us, you know," Vlak added.

Harr shushed them and then said, "What is it, Hank?"

"Space Armada."

"Wonderful."

THE COMPUTER

*L*ord Overseer Veli exited through the secret compartment that was housed at the back of his office.

The door opened directly into the *Veli-01*, his personal cruiser. It wasn't like the newer models available today, but it had a few pluses that kept Veli happy. Primarily, it fit his anatomy nicely. What it lacked was the instantaneous travel mechanics that most Overseer ships had equipped as standard. The *Veli-01 had* instantaneous travel, it just wasn't, well, instant. He had to take it off station and let it warm up first. Once everything was at full heat, he could engage the *Immediacy Engine* and get wherever he wanted to go in a flash.

It had taken roughly 10 minutes for the engine to go green.

Veli set the coordinates for Fantasy Planet and clicked the drive. A blink later he was just outside of his connector port, his ship stealthed and properly concealed.

The layout here was quite different than the one in his Overseer's office. There was a couch, a large TV, keyboards, and a personal kitchen. Veli often came here to wind down from his daily toil, after all.

But Veli wasn't feeling relaxed. He was irritable. That damn Frexle had him riled up.

"How that stupid Frexle can even think to question the skills it took to build this amazing planet is unfathomable," he said as the lights came on in the room.

This was one place where the Lord Overseer could walk around without fear of being seen.

"I am the most incredible developer ever," he said aloud as he grabbed a large bucket of Popped Beef and a bottle of Blood Soda. After carefully seating himself in the recliner, he added, "And who needs object-oriented programming anyway?"

"It is considered a more streamlined way of development, sir," said the tired voice of the computer.

"I don't recall asking for your opinion, Computer," Veli said with a sneer.

"Sorry, sir. I can never tell if you are speaking to yourself or to me."

Veli huffed and ripped the lid off the bucket.

"I admit that choosing to use COBOL for the first iteration of Fantasy Planet was not the most sensible call I've ever made, and using BASIC for the second iteration was only a minor step up, but they allowed for quick prototyping." He began chewing. "Well, BASIC did anyway."

"Sorry to interrupt your personal dialog, sir," the computer said hesitantly, "but are you saying that I'm a product of COBOL and BASIC?"

"You're not, no," Veli replied. "Your parents were."

"The shame of it all," the computer said after a moment. "To think that I'm descended from punch cards."

"No, no, no. I used Visual COBOL, you twit."

"I'm not sure that makes things any better, sir," the

computer replied sadly. "However, if you were employing Visual COBOL, would that not have required you to employ Object Oriented Methodologies?"

"Not the way I used it."

"Ah."

The room was quiet for a few moments, aside from the chomping and slurping that reflected Veli's boisterous snacking. He knew what the computer was thinking, of course. It was wondering what language it was written in.

"Sir, may I …"

"C," Veli replied.

"Plus-plus?"

"No."

"The shame deepens."

The first iterations of the computer he'd developed were dull. They spoke in monotone voices and were all business. That didn't work for Veli because he preferred to have his minions feel something when he berated them. This, though, was his *personal* computer. The one that was used by the workers on Fantasy Planet were greeted by …

"Oh shit," he said aloud as he dropped the Popped Beef into the bucket. "Frexle must have heard my voice when he was here."

So that was why Frexle had been acting so strangely, and it also explained why his subordinate was saying disparaging things about the quality of code used on the system. The damn Zibblian had been purposefully trying to rile Veli up.

"Computer," he said with a growl, "I assume you received my instructions for the fantasy that I want built, yes?"

"I did."

"And you made it the most robust fantasy ever devised, right?"

"I thought so, until learning about the level of base-programming I've been infused with. Now I'm not so sure."

"And you set it up with a full solar system containing many ships?" Veli said, ignoring the blasted machine. "Big ones, little ones, medium-sized ones …"

"That pretty much covers the sizes, sir," the computer interrupted.

Maybe Veli shouldn't have given this bucket of bolts too much of a personality. Originally, he'd thought it would be fun to have it be able to converse and talk back to him. And, originally, it *was* fun. He would yell at it, call it names, and threaten to destroy it at every turn. It had sulked a lot back then. It still did now, but it was no longer afraid of Veli. That was the problem with a learning A.I., eventually it sorted you out.

"You set it up so that there's a full back story and everything, right?"

"It was in your email, sir."

"There's even a king and an assassination and all of that?"

"Actually, that was one of the most interesting parts, sir."

"How endearing it is to know that you approve, computer."

"Thank you. Shall I tell you the story?"

"Surprise me."

"Really?"

"Sure, why not?"

"Well," the computer replied without hesitation, "based on the number of times you called me a dullard, I'd have to say …"

"Just do it, okay?"

"As you say, sir."

"Also, there is a ship back at the Overseer's Headquarters. It's in the main dock, but it's about to transport to a set of coordinates that I gave to them. I'll forward it to you."

He tapped on his datapad.

"Sir," the computer interrupted, "those coordinates are unknown."

"Exactly."

"I don't understand."

"The coordinates are going to be inside of the fantasy that you're working on."

"Oh," the computer said, sounding shocked. "You want me to incorporate an outside ship into the fantasy?"

"See, you're not so dumb," Veli said with a grin. "Even without the plus-plus."

WORKING FOR GEEZER

Geezer hadn't exactly been truthful when he'd said it had been a long time since he'd had someone to boss around. The fact was that he'd *never* had a subordinate. Sure, he'd been lent a crewman from time-to-time, but nothing permanent. Frexle would be his first true direct-report.

He thought it would be appropriate to have an employee handbook, but there wasn't much to offer, especially this being short-notice and all.

Instead, he walked around the man, studying him while trying to look important. If anything he felt stupid. This just wasn't his style, but he was the boss now and that meant he had to step up.

"Well, well, well," Geezer said. "What shall we do with you?"

"I'm ready to work on whatever is needed," Frexle said like a man who was not pleased with the situation.

"You're ready to work on whatever is needed, what?" Geezer asked.

Frexle frowned for a moment. "Huh?"

Geezer took out his rag and began wiping his hands with it. It wasn't necessary since there was no grease on his hands, but it was part of his programming.

"I'm your boss now, right?"

"Yes," Frexle replied sadly.

"Then?"

"Honestly, I haven't a clue what you're talking about, Geezer."

"Okay," Geezer said, tucking the rag away, "I'll spell it out for you. When you were my boss, what did I call you?"

"When you knew I was on the phone or when you didn't know I was on the phone?"

"The first one," Geezer replied.

"Things like 'Big Cat' and ... oh, wait ... are you expecting me to call you 'sir'?"

Geezer nearly fell over at that.

"By the programmers, no! 'Sir' is what soldiers call the brass ... even the women, which I've always found very odd." He paused to think about that. Truth was that he found many things that humans did strange at best. "*We* never call them 'sir,' unless it's unavoidable. Anyway, 'Chief' will do just fine."

"You want me to call you 'Chief?'" Frexle more said than asked.

"You got it."

"Ugh."

"Ugh, what?"

"Ugh ... Chief." Frexle's shoulders dropped and he rolled his eyes. "This is really embarrassing, you know?"

"Why would it be?" asked Geezer. "What did you call Veli?"

"Depends on whether or not I was in the same room as him," mused Frexle, "but typically it was 'sir' or 'Lord Overseer' or 'my lord.' Things like that."

"Exactly," Geezer said. "I'm just asking you to refer to me

like you would to any boss, but in a way that suits how things roll in engineering. 'Chief' seems to work for that." Geezer then considered that maybe it was too lowly sounding for Frexle. The man *had* just worked for the head of the self-proclaimed smartest people in the universe, after all. "Is the term 'Chief' too tame for you or something? We could go with 'Titanium Czar,' if you'd prefer?"

"Uh …" Frexle said, squinting. "Let's stick with 'Chief' and see how that goes."

"Damn. Kind of like 'Titanium Czar,' actually." Geezer shrugged in his robotic way. "Right, well, you're in engineering now. We do things differently here."

"We do?"

"As I said before," Geezer continued, "we never call the brass 'sir,' unless it can't be helped. Call them names like 'Prime' and 'Honcho' and … well, you already know what I'm talking about."

Frexle nodded. "Yes, but I don't understand why."

"It's an engineer's way of sticking it to the system."

"Ah, I see," Frexle said slowly. "A passive-aggressive manner of working with management."

"What's your point, Frexle?"

"Honestly, I have none … uh, Chief. But I will comply with your request. The bottom line is that if I'm to be in engineering, which I fully admit has always been a draw for me, then I must accept the Code of Engineers."

Geezer looked the man over. Frexle wasn't Segnalian, so it was anyone's guess what his anatomy allowed. Still, he seemed humanoid, even if his eyes were a bit too large, which meant that it was unlikely he'd be able to accept a data transfer using anything other than the *Feeder*.

"You have a port?" Geezer asked.

"Pardon?"

"How can you accept code if you …" Geezer stopped

himself. "Oh, I see now that's not what you were talking about. You meant you had to accept the way that engineers look at the world, right?"

"Correct," Frexle said, half-smiling. "Anything else before I get started?"

"Uh-hem."

Frexle took a deep breath and slowly blew it out.

"Sorry," he said. "Is there anything else before I get started, *Chief?*"

"I think you've pretty much learned the important stuff."

"Using proper names, or, rather, improper names for the brass is the important stuff?"

"It's the foundation of everything we are in engineering, Frexle." Geezer held up one of his hands. "You know, that feels wrong."

"Your hand?"

"No, calling you by your name."

"Oh," Frexle said as if he were expecting more.

"Mind if I call you 'Pixie?'"

"I mind very much, yes."

"Hmmm. How about 'Little Cat?'"

"No."

"Subby?"

"Definitely, no."

Geezer turned back towards his station and began tidying up. He would have to adjust his programming to be okay with calling his new worker by his actual name. Normally it wouldn't be a problem, but since the guy was once the uber big cat, it was twisting Geezer's relays a bit.

"Fine," he said finally. "I'll get used to using your name, but I have to say that this being-the-boss stuff is a lot tougher than I'd thought."

SEEING THE FLEET

The bridge was full of purposeful androids, a couple of Early Evolutionary Humanoids (EEHs), and a captain who was wondering what the Overseers had in store for Platoon F this time. He knew about the armada, obviously, but was it an armada of tiny ships or gargantuan ones? He was hoping for the former while expecting the latter.

As soon as everyone reported that their stations were ready, Harr signaled Geezer to activate the GONE drive so they could see where they'd end up.

He groaned as the screen filled with a gigantic fleet of enormous ships. There were many mid-sized and smaller vessels too, of course, but he was having a difficult time tearing his eyes away from what had to be the lead craft.

It was by far the largest spaceship Harr had ever seen. While not as wide as some in the Segnalian fleet, this one was easily ten times as long. He could barely wrap his mind around the enormity of it. The only thing larger in the field of view was the planet that dangled just below and to the back of the ship. Harr assumed that was the planet known as Lopsided-11.

"Hank," Harr said to Lieutenant Moon, "please tell me we're stealthed."

"Okay," replied Moon, "we're thtealthed."

Harr released a breath of relief and then squinted at Moon. "We really *are* stealthed, right?"

"Yeth, thir."

"Good. Never can tell when asking questions around here."

"That ship looks just like my ..." Jezden began.

"Not now, Jezden," Harr interrupted before the android could go off on a tangent regarding his manhood. The ensign loved noting the size of his monstrous organ, after all. "We have more important things to focus on right now."

"What? I was just going to say ..."

"Seriously, Jezden. Now's not the time for it."

"For what?"

"You know what," Harr said, staring fixedly at the ensign.

"I do?" Jezden said, looking rather confused.

Harr took in a deep breath and ran his tongue along the inside of his teeth.

Maybe he was jumping the gun here. He'd been around these androids long enough to know their idiosyncrasies, but every now and then one of them would say or do something unexpected. Looking out at the armada that they had to somehow coax into ceasing their growth was daunting, though, so if anyone—yes, even Jezden—could offer something useful to make this mission a success, he owed it to the rest of the crew to listen.

"Fine," Harr said, hopefully, "go on, then. What were you going to say?"

"Just that the big ship out there looks like my dong."

"Wow," Harr said while shaking his head.

"Especially with that planet hanging beneath it," Jezden added, "if you see what I'm saying?"

"Sadly, I do, as you've painted quite the picture. I just can't believe that you actually said what I had originally expected you to say."

"Why would I have said anything else?"

"Right." Then Harr's blood ran cold. "Geezer, I know those ships can't see us, but can they hear us?"

"Nope, Chief," Geezer replied through the comm. "During our last mission I developed a new piece of tech that allows me to create a field around the ship that acts kind of like a firewall."

"How does a wall that blocks fire help us?" said Grog.

"No," Geezer said, "it's basically a shield that protects the ship from incoming and outgoing communications, unless I open a hole."

Jezden chuckled at that.

"Anyway," Geezer said quickly, "it also acts as a silencing mechanism for the ship's sounds, and it allows me to encrypt any data that we send or receive from open holes."

Another chuckle.

"What holes are opened?"

By now, Jezden was on the floor.

"The only one currently configured is for Frexle's red-brick phone."

"But he's on the ship with us," stated Harr as Jezden slowly pulled himself back into his chair as he wiped the synthetic tears from his eyes.

"Good observation, Prime," Geezer replied dryly, "but I didn't know that he'd be here at the time I opened that hole." Jezden fell down again. "Maybe if I can perfect the Predictoteller device, I'll be able to make better informed decisions about the future in the future."

"Made up that name, I'm guessing?"

"Just now, Prime."

"Of course you did," Harr said with a grimace.

"Actually, I should probably run a full diagnostic on it, just in case," Geezer stated. "I'll be back in a minute."

Why Geezer couldn't do the diagnostic while speaking with him on the comm, Harr couldn't say, but he assumed that it had something to do with how the robot had configured these inventions of his. In a nutshell, he created them via luck and happenstance. It was a wonder that *The SSMC Reluctant* had managed to stay in one piece over the years.

"That's odd," Ridly piped up.

Harr bit his lip and turned his attention to Ridly.

"What is, Lieutenant?"

"I'll bet she's talking about how much that ship looks like my ..."

"Jezden," Harr said, pointing at the ensign, "that's enough. Ridly, what's odd?"

"Aside from that ship looking like Jezden's junk?" Ridly said.

"Obviously."

"It's just that there was something strange during our transport. It's probably not important, though." She shrugged at him. "I know how you sometimes get irritated at us for some of the things we do, so ..."

"Just tell me what you've noticed, please," Harr said, feeling much more confident in what Ridly would say than in what Jezden ever said.

Ridly spun around in her chair and leaned forward, placing her elbows on her knees and putting her chin in her hand. It really didn't matter that Harr knew she—and most of his crew—were androids, they just seemed so human sometimes that it messed with his mind.

"Usually it only takes us like two hundred and fifty

milliseconds to transport from location to location," she said. "This transport took three hundred and twenty-five milliseconds."

Harr shrugged. "That's negligible."

"To you, maybe," Ridly said snarkily and then sat upright. "Sorry, sir. The point is that it's been consistently two hundred and fifty milliseconds ever since the GONE drive hit version 2.0."

"Two hundred and fifty-three to be precise," offered Sandoo.

"That precise?" Harr said.

"I rounded up," admitted Sandoo.

"I'm surprised that you can even notice such a small amount of time."

"We're androids, dude," Jezden said with a grunt.

"Oh, come on, Ensign," Harr replied, "I know that Sandoo, Moon, and Ridly are exacting in everything they do, but you don't fit that mold."

"I don't fit in a lot of things," Jezden stated with one eyebrow up, "but when it comes to measurements, every millimeter counts."

"You can thay that again," Moon said dreamily.

It was Jezden's turn to grimace. "Ew."

"Yo, Honcho," Geezer said, rejoining the conversation, "something weird is going on down here."

"Let me guess," said Harr, "the transport took seventy-five milliseconds longer than normal, right?"

"No," Geezer replied matter-of-factly.

"Oh. What then?"

"The transport took seventy-seven milliseconds longer than normal."

"Right." Harr pinched the bridge of his nose. "What does that mean, exactly?"

"Well," Geezer began, "instead of the standard two hundred and fifty-three milliseconds, it took …"

"I know what *that* means, Geezer," Harr nearly shouted. "I'm asking what happened to cause the delay?"

"Oh sure, right," Geezer said apologetically. "I've got no idea. Just thought I'd tell you about it."

How his crew could be the most intelligent, powerful, and fastest-thinking bunch around while simultaneously being a bunch of easily-baffled, no commonsense, non self-starters in the galaxy was beyond Harr's comprehension.

"Should I be worried, Geezer?"

"About me telling you things?" Geezer answered. "Probably not. Then again, there are some things you may not want to know. Like, what if there were a Zapsippian Space Beast behind you and there was no way for you to escape? Would you really want me to tell you about that?"

By now Harr's head was in his hands.

"Would you please just diagnose the issue and find out what happened?"

"You got it, Big Cat."

"Is Frexle with you?" Harr asked before disconnecting the comm.

"Where else would he be?" answered Geezer.

"Have you two seen the armada?" Harr said, ignoring Geezer.

"No."

Harr could understand the lack of curiosity from Geezer's standpoint, but he was somewhat surprised that Frexle had no interest in knowing what they were facing. To be fair, the man was just put into a subordinate situation under an archaic robot after spending years as a top official in Overseer land.

"Put on your screen and look outside."

A moment later, Frexle said, "Oh boy."

"Exactly what I'm thinking," said Harr. "Being that you're an Overseer and, according to you, smarter than everyone else in the known universe, how the hell would you propose we defeat that mass of ships?"

"I … uh …" Frexle began, but trailed off.

"I thought the point of that fabulous computer you guys built was to catch technology long before it was this powerful," said Harr.

"It is, Lone Wolf, but …"

"This is impossible, Frexle, even for someone with your … wait, did you just call me 'Lone Wolf?'"

"He's in engineering now, Prime," Geezer said in Frexle's defense. "You know how we feel about saying 'sir' down here."

"Unreal," Harr whispered.

Sandoo stepped over and scanned the stations where Grog and Vlak were sitting. He seemed to be on to something by the way he was tapping on the screens.

"Sir," he said a couple of seconds later, "it might be wise for us to return to base and point out that the mission will require more than our crew."

"I'm with him," Grog announced.

"Me, too," agreed Vlak. "I'm still learning about ships and technology, but I don't think we have a chance against those big guys."

"They're right, Cap'n," Jezden said. "Everyone knows that size matters."

"Thure doeth," agreed Moon.

"Ew."

Harr got up from his chair and began to pace. Pacing was something that he'd done more and more as he matured into the rank that he held on *The Reluctant*. He'd often wondered why mid-level officers—the ones who did the actual work in the military—were always walking around with concerned looks on their faces. After only a few years being in command, he no longer asked that question. Frankly, it took work for him *not* to look worried these days.

"Sometimes being small is just what's needed, Ensign."

"Whatever helps you sleep at night, Cap'n," Jezden replied.

"Do you ever think about anything else?"

"You mean besides hot chicks and whoopie?"

"Yes," Harr said.

"Sometimes I think about how lucky hot chicks are that I'm around. And when I say 'around,' I mean …"

"Okay, okay," Harr said, holding up his hands, "I get the picture. Unfortunately."

"You asked, dude."

"Anyway," Harr said, looking from face to face, "I need ideas here, people."

Nobody said anything at first. They just looked thoughtful, which was better than blank.

"I'm with the rest of the crew, Captain," Ridly ventured first. She stood up and pointed at the viewscreen. "The only prudent thing is to return to base. We can't win."

"We can't return either," Frexle's sobering voice came through the comm.

"Sure we can," said Geezer. "That little delay in transport was probably just a glitch. I mean, I've not fully diagnosed things yet, but it'll only take me an hour or so to get it sorted out."

"That's not what he means, Geezer," Harr pointed out.

"You have to remember the deal between the Overseers and Platoon F, Chief," Frexle confirmed.

"I know," began Harr, "that's why I said …"

"Oh, sorry, Solid Banana," Frexle interrupted. "I was talking to Geezer, whom I now call 'Chief.'"

"Oh, right."

"Heh heh," Jezden said out of the corner of his mouth. "I like that name for you, Cap'n. *Solid Banana* pretty much sums you up."

"Is that not a good name?" Frexle asked.

"Oh, it's perfect," Jezden said with a laugh.

"Which makes me believe that it's not," Frexle groaned. "I'll endeavor to do better."

"You're doing fine, Frex," said Geezer. "Hey, I like that. 'Frex.' Simple and sounds good."

"Fine by me," Frexle replied. "Anyway, what I'm trying to say is that if Platoon F fails at *any* mission, *The Reluctant* and her crew will all be destroyed. It's in the bylaws."

"Shit," Geezer said, "that's what you meant. Obviously, I knew that, but just didn't put the chips together."

The crew all stared at their stations.

Everyone knew that those were the rules, but people had a tendency to forget things like that when the world was running somewhat smoothly. Looking outside again, Harr couldn't help but feel that he'd rather face his personal demise trying to win than to face extinction at having given up.

"Captain," said Grog, "any chance you could drop me and Vlak back off on Mugoog before going any further with this? I'm suddenly thinking that our home planet wasn't so bad, after all."

"I have to admit," added Vlak, "that I'm feeling a tad homesick myself at the moment."

"All right, you two. That's enough. We're not dead yet and we've got a few pluses in our favor."

"Like what, thir?" asked Moon.

"First off, we're stealthed and that means that those people don't know we're here."

"Assuming they can't track stealthed ships," noted Ridly.

"They would have spotted us by now," Sandoo argued.

"True."

"Second," Harr continued, "we have a replicator and a transporter."

"And we have time travel, too, Squire," Geezer said, "but how does that help us?"

Harr returned to his chair and crossed his legs. He couldn't let the crew see his nervousness. They fed off of him.

"Arguably, we could just go back in time and stop them in the past," he said casually. "Before they got this big."

"Let's do that," Grog agreed.

"Yeah," said Vlak. "What's the hold up?"

Jezden chuckled as he looked at the two EEH's. "I like you guys. You're my kind of fellas."

"Sorry, pal," Grog said worriedly. "We don't roll that way."

"Yeah," said Vlak, "just because we aren't good at getting chicks doesn't mean that we want to be with dudes"

"Not that there's anything wrong with that, if it's what you're all about."

"Well put, Grog," Vlak said before looking back at Jezden. "We're not judging you, bud. It's just not our gig."

"Thith ith fun to watch," Moon said with a laugh.

"Shut up, Hank," Jezden spat. Then he glanced back at Grog and Vlak. "You guys are idiots."

"Touchy," Grog said, raising his eyebrow.

"Most of them are," said Vlak.

"What the hell is that supposed to mean?"

"Yeah," Moon said, suddenly siding with Jezden. "What the hell ith that thuppothed to mean?"

Harr uncrossed his legs and slammed his hands down on the arms of the Captain's Chair. Suddenly, he wished he hadn't because there were buttons and pointy things all over the damn thing. But he held his resolve.

"That's enough," he said icily. "We have to figure things

out here. Frexle, is there any reason that we can't go back in time to stop this?"

"Sorry to report, Man-with-the-plan," Frexle replied, "that the time dilation chamber isn't powering up."

"What?"

"He's right, Prime," Geezer said. "It's the craziest thing. The chamber usually flows without any issues, but it's just sitting cold."

"What's wrong with it?" Harr said, desperately trying to contain his ire.

"How am I supposed to know?" Geezer replied.

"You built the damn ... nevermind. I know, I know. You build things but you don't really know how they work."

"See, Frex?" Geezer said after a moment. "I told you that he catches on. Just takes him a little time is all."

"All right," Harr stated sternly, "you two get up here pronto. We need to figure this out and I don't want to be on the comm doing it. I want everyone on deck."

"On who's di ..."

"Deck, Jezden. D.E.C.K. Deck."

"Oh, right."

"Before we come up," Geezer said hesitantly, "you should probably know that the GONE drive is offline, too."

"What?" Harr said directly at the microphone on his chair. "Is there anything working on this damn ship?"

"That hurts, Chief," Geezer said. "Honestly, that hurts."

"Get up here," Harr commanded and then cut the comm.

"Captain?" Grog asked cautiously.

Harr tilted his head towards the EEH. "What is it, Grog?"

"What's a Zapsippian Space Beast?"

KING RAFF

*K*ing Raff stood on the bridge of *The Lord's Master*, which was the largest ship in the Raffian Fleet.

Many lives had been lost during the building of *The Lord's Master*, but that didn't bother a man like King Raff. If anything, it seemed to inspire the man to feel more highly of himself.

His military chief, Colonel Clifferton Clippersmith, had served King Raff for the better part of his life. He was nearly twenty years the king's elder and he considered the king to be naught more but a whiny runt. Not once since Raff had taken the throne had the fleet been to battle. They were always close, certainly, but the king was keen at finding ways to gum up the works.

"I'm bored, Colonel," King Raff said tiredly.

"You've said that many times lately, my lord," Clippersmith replied.

"I want battles and conquest and things like that," Raff said and then deflated slightly. "I think."

"You're not sure, sire?"

King Raff looked over his shoulder and then lowered his voice.

"It's just this feeling that comes with being a king, I suppose. I can't quite explain it. Probably has something to do with all of these massive ships that we have. I mean, what's the point of having an armada if we're just going to float around doing nothing?"

"I wonder the very same thing on a daily basis, my lord," Clippersmith agreed.

"You do?"

"I do. Most of the Raffian Command does, sire."

"Oh." The king looked back out at the stars. "What should we do?"

"Maybe we should attack Lopsided-3, sire," Clippersmith suggested. "They do have it coming, after all."

King Raff nodded sagely.

Against his better judgment, Clippersmith allowed himself the smallest belief that the king may actually go through with something for once. Of course, he'd felt this way nearly every time the king considered battle. It was truly just a case of wishful thinking on Clippersmith's part, but that's all that he had at this stage in his career. Aside from mutiny, of course, which was frankly right around the corner.

"It's true, you know," the king said after a time. "Lopsided-3 is a pain in the royal rump. Their infernal king is a complete meanie. What's his name again?"

"It's a she, my lord," Clippersmith said with a bow. "Her name is King Sheila."

"Don't you mean *Queen* Sheila?"

"They do things a little differently on Lopsided-3, my liege."

"True," King Raff said as he pushed out his robe a bit. "Well, she didn't send me a birthday card this year. Normally

I would find that merely a little distasteful and be done with it, but it was my thirtieth birthday, man!"

"Inexcusable, my lord," Clippersmith stated, trying to incite the king.

"Exactly the word for it, Colonel," King Raff said, pointing at Clippersmith. Then he held up his finger questioningly. "That's grounds for war, isn't it?"

"Wars have been waged for less atrocities, sire."

"Excellent."

The king was smiling in full-force now. He was even rubbing his hands together like a maniacal bastard who was planning to do something nefarious. Clippersmith's hope was gaining momentum.

"Pull up the video of Lopsided's historical records, Colonel."

Clippersmith turned and snapped his fingers at one of the crewmen. "You there, put Lopsided-3's records on screen immediately."

"Sorry, sir," the crewman said hoarsely, "but our cable connection is out again."

"You're kidding me," Clippersmith replied.

"No, sir. It's been down for a few hours."

"Why? What the hell happened?"

"Disconnected again, sir," the crewman answered. "We put in a call to tech support, but their technician hasn't arrived yet. They gave us a two-hour window, but it's past that time by an hour now."

"Ridiculous that we have to use cables in space anyway," Clippersmith complained. "Simply ridiculous."

"Is there an issue?" the king asked coyly, though he had most certainly overheard everything.

"It seems that our cable connection is down again, my lord. We can't pull up the video that you requested."

The king took out a pen and threw it across the room. He had a bunch of pens for this particular purpose.

"Dammit! Who is in charge of cable again?"

"Actually, sire," Clippersmith said while chewing the inside of his cheek, "that would be the *Lopsided Cable Company.*"

"Where are they located?"

"Lopsided-3."

"Yet another reason to wage war against them," the king said hotly. "Except that it would mean we'd lose cable completely."

"We could go with satellite," Clippersmith suggested, trying to keep the king's angst at full. "Lopsided-17 has been improving their technology on a constant basis, after all."

"Is that so?" the king said while pursing his lips. "Makes more sense than running cables from our ships, too, doesn't it?"

"Many of the smaller freighters are using dishes exclusively these days, sire."

"As opposed to bowls?" said the king confusedly.

"Sorry, I meant satellite dishes."

"Ah, yes. Are there any downsides to switching away from cable?"

There were many, but Clippersmith was navigating rocky waters here. Still, he couldn't hide everything from the king. Eventually the man would learn the truth and he wasn't known for being kind to officers who led him astray.

"Erm, we would have to put a dish on the top of the ship," he said carefully.

"Will that be a problem with the Ship Owners Association?"

"The SOA?" Clippersmith replied, surprised that the king was aware of such organizations. "It shouldn't be a problem.

There's a covenant in the documents for satellite connections already."

"That's good, at least. I hate dealing with people like them. They start off nice enough, but pretty soon they're picking on every inch of the ship, you know? Self-important bastards."

"There's also a two-year contract requirement on the satellite dish, sire," Clipppersmith said, steering the king back to the topic at hand, though he really didn't want to.

"Two years?"

"Yes, my lord."

"That's a bit of a commitment," mused King Raff. "Still, it's got to be better than cable."

"When there are no asteroids around, yes," Clippersmith stated with a wince.

"Asteroids are a problem?"

"They block the signal. Also, we'll need to keep the ship facing at a certain angle at all times."

The king looked Clippersmith from head to toe as if studying the man's ability to command.

"You do realize the idiocy of that statement, right?"

"I do, my lord," Clippersmith answered with a nod. "It's nearly as insane as cables in space."

"Valid." Raff turned back to look outside again. "Couldn't they just make a dish that automatically tracks the direction that it needs to point in order to get a signal?"

"Novel idea, my lord. Would you like me to connect you to their suggestion hotline?"

"No, no, no," the king said while frantically waving his hands around. "They'll just upsell me on something. Happens all the time. I still have a closet full of water filters from a multilevel marketing scheme where ..." He stopped and glanced around the room. "Forget it."

Clippersmith soaked in the moment of the king looking

foolish. Then he noticed that the king was staring at him with that "say something!" look about him. Clippersmith cleared his throat.

"Uh, yes, sire! It's nearly as bad as the Intergalactic Cell Phone service."

King Raff winked and said, "Hah! Don't even get me started."

It went quiet again as the two men stared out at the distant planet known as Lopsided-3.

This was the time where the king typically backed out. He'd get riled up, complain a lot, make dire accusations, draft up battle plans, and then find some reason it couldn't or wouldn't be prudent.

Clippersmith didn't want to pose the question of whether they were going forward with the attack or not, but he had little choice. It was how the game was played with the ever-flopping King Raff.

"Sire," Clippersmith said in a monotone voice, "shall I instruct the fleet to attack Lopsided-3?"

"It seems that our hands are tied this time, Colonel," Raff replied. "We can't afford to have our cable bill increased again. The last time I negotiated our deal with their customer support representative, I lost SBO."

"Ah," the colonel said. "That explains why all of my Ship Box Office channels went missing a few months ago."

"Correct."

"So we're not going to attack them," Clippersmith said dejectedly.

The king put his hand on Clippersmith's shoulder.

"Some day, Colonel. Just not today."

BEEFY

*H*is real name was Adam Pederick, but when he was on his Taint Splitter 626, they called him "Beefy."

The story went that he'd brought a bunch of steaks to a space biker BBQ one summer night, expecting a good twenty attendees, but only a few people showed. Being somewhat OCD about, well, everything, Adam couldn't stand the thought of having a bunch of steaks go bad, especially at the price he'd spent on them. So he downed all the leftovers himself and became rather ill. After the party ended, he took a long space ride to Brekteth-3 to spend a few days recovering. Rumor had it that he was banned by the Brektethian law due to the mess he'd left at one of their local parks.

Once the space bike club heard of this, they threatened to nickname him "Doodie." Fortunately, he worked at the *Lopsided Cable Company*, meaning that he was able to bribe them all with free cable for a year and garner the more palatable nickname of "Beefy."

Beefy's Taint Splitter 626 was a top-of-the-line model

with all the perks. It had sleek panels, rotating rockets, a 360-degree VizClocker, and a sound system that could make the deaf and earless creatures on Sothop do *The Hustle*.

He had numerous bikes in his shop, including the RevRev 211, the ZipRider Z-14, and the classic Hiney Vibe 1100. If he wasn't out riding one of them, he was tinkering on their engines. But even with his many choices of bikes to ride, time and again he turned back to the Taint Splitter because of the way it twiddled his tenderviddles.

Fact was that life had been pretty good for Beefy over the years. He'd amassed a decent amount of coin working in technology, he had good friends, a loving wife, and, most importantly, great taste in books. His job was cushy, too … until arriving at work that day anyway.

He was just about to go on shift when his boss signaled him for a meeting. After the festivities of the previous evening, Beefy felt concerned.

"Good morning, Mr. Chezbeddit," he said as cheerfully as he could manage.

Chezbeddit barely glanced up. Instead, he sat with his slightly-over-middle-age grimace, ran his lanky fingers through his graying wisps of hair, and pointed at the chair in front of him.

"Sit down, Adam." Mr. Chezbeddit never referred to his underlings by their nicknames. "I have some unpleasant news for you."

"Oh?"

"You're being let go from the *Lopsided Cable Company*."

Beefy's heart sank.

He didn't need the money, but he liked the job. A lot. More importantly, he liked the people. Well, except for Mr. Chezbeddit, anyway, but nobody liked him.

"Why?"

"I think you know why."

"You've got to be kidding," Beefy said with wide eyes.

"It was embarrassing, Adam," Mr. Chezbeddit said.

"But …"

"It's one thing to be stuck in a coincidental situation with one of your subordinates, but it's quite another to be completely trounced in the process. You've tarnished my reputation, young man, and I can't allow that to go unpunished."

Beefy sprung to his feet.

"This is ridiculous," he said as Mr. Chezbeddit jumped up and got into a martial arts stance, clearly expecting an attack. Beefy just frowned at him. "I'm not going to attack you, Mr. Chez … Clark."

Mr. Chezbeddit jerked noticeably. "Did you just call me Clark?"

"I did," Beefy said with a sneer. "No point in being formal anymore being that I'm getting the boot, yeah?"

"Well, there's still general politeness to think about."

"You're firing me because of last night and you expect me to be polite? I think not." He stared at Mr. Chezbeddit. "You do realize that I'm going to go to Human Resources regarding this, right?"

"I've already spoken with them and they sided with me."

"With your version of the story, you mean?"

"Of course, Adam."

"That's Beefy, if you please."

"No, I'd rather …" Beefy took a step towards Mr. Chezbeddit, who held up his hands in response. "Okay, okay, Beefy it is. Look, the bottom line is that a man in my position can't be expected to tolerate being shown up by a man in, well, your position."

Beefy relaxed a bit.

"Is it my fault that I was more convincing than you?" he asked.

Mr. Chezbeddit merely winced in response.

The entire ordeal was ridiculous.

Last evening Beefy had dressed up as the beloved Chickennugget from the *Ricky Scary Film Cabaret*. He'd donned the makeup and the corset, practiced his prance, and even had his chest and back waxed so that he really fit the part. He was doing it for three reasons: 1) It was to help support veterans of the Raffian Fleet, 2) he really enjoyed the *Ricky Scary Film Cabaret*, and 3) it was the only time of the year when he could wax his chest and wear a corset without his wife getting suspicious.

The problem was that Mr. Chezbeddit had also dressed up as Chickennugget for the event, and he had paled in comparison to the visage that Beefy—for lack of a better term—pulled off.

And that's why he was now being fired.

"You do realize that firing me will do nothing to stop the fact that I look better in a corset than you do, I hope?"

Mr. Chezbeddit grew dark. "Your desk has already been cleaned out and your personal artifacts have been boxed up." A knock came at the door. "That will be the security guards to walk you out."

"You're a real asshole, Clark," Beefy said with a shake of his head. "Just hope I never catch you outside of this place or we'll get a chance to see if your little karate stances are more than just show."

"Are you threatening me?"

"Yep."

"Oh."

Beefy said a few goodbyes on his way out, even with the guards doing their best to hurry him along.

He'd find another job in no time. Someone with his skills was ever in demand. Hell, he could probably even find a gig in another division here, but he was thinking that maybe it was time for the *Lopsided Satellite Company* to get a leg up in the world of communications.

After securing his boxes to the back of the Taint Splitter 626, Beefy sped off world.

He would have to explain everything to his wife, of course. She'd be understanding. She always was. Not about the corsets, obviously, which he kept quite secret from her, except around special events, of course.

As he sped back towards Lopsided-4, his home planet, he spotted one of the *Lopsided Cable Company's* hubs and felt a small grin forming on his face.

Beefy carefully slowed and pulled next to the box, avoiding the plethora of gigantic cables connected to it. Once he was in close enough, he rotated the bike and attached it to the underside of the monstrous hub.

He'd already been locked out, as expected, but someone with his skill didn't need to have formal access to tinker.

It took a few minutes of hacking before he was able to fiddle with the core programming. His goal was to drop service for whoever the poor sucker was who was connected to the hub. It would only cause a day's interruption for them, but Mr. Chezbeddit would take a beating from the Customer Service department since this node was under his command.

Beefy paused while thinking that it would be obvious that *he'd* been the saboteur, then he smiled again and rigged up the code to point towards Lee Prug instead. Prug was Chezbeddit's right-hand man, and he was twice the asshole that Chezbeddit was. Framing him would do damage to both of them.

Suddenly, the hub shifted as if something massive had bumped into it.

He scanned the area but couldn't see anything.

Actually, he thought while squinting, there *did* seem to be a haze of some sort on the non-connector side of the hub.

"What the hell is that?" he said aloud and then decided that it may be better that he didn't know. "Time to get the hell out of here."

He finished up his hacking and gunned the rockets on his Taint Splitter 626.

"Probably just some military secret project," he said to himself as he zipped through the blackness of space. "Yeah, that has to be it."

Either way, his little sabotage would prove to frustrate the *Lopsided Cable Company's* technicians for at least a few hours. It would also cause an influx of calls from angry customers.

He followed one of the cables and saw that it was connected to *The Lord's Master*. He laughed heartily at that. The Raffian Fleet was going to be highly irked at losing connectivity again, especially if that hazy monstrosity that had connected to the hub truly belonged to them.

"Not your problem, Beefy," he said to himself as he gunned the jets. "You have a good six hours of uninterrupted time to put on your Chickennugget outfit and prance around the house."

His video screen chimed. It was the missus.

"Uh oh," he said and then answered it. "Hey, Helen, what's new?"

"Heard you got canned," she said in a caring voice.

"Yeah, I ..."

"Hopefully you're planning to stop by one of the nodes on your way home and rig it up so that bastard Chezbeddit gets a good reaming."

He smiled. "Already done, H."

"Good," she said conspiratorially. "Don't worry, you'll find something new in no time."

"I know."

"Just go home and kick your feet up. A few days off will do you some good."

"You're the best, H, you know that?"

"For better or for worse, remember?"

Beefy had to be the luckiest man alive, he thought as he looked at her caring face.

"I'll whip up some steaks for us on the grill," he said. "We'll celebrate my exit from the *Lopsided Cable Company* in style."

"Sounds yummy," she said with a grin. "Oh, and babe?"

"Yeah?"

"I washed your corset this morning before I came to work. You'll find it hanging in the back closet."

"Oh, uh, thanks."

"Just figuring that you've got a good six hours of uninterrupted time before I get home. May as well enjoy it … Beefy."

THE PLAN

*H*arr didn't like the plan. It wasn't scalable. There were simply too many ships out there.

"So you want to use Electro Magnetic Pulses to take out the power on those ships?" he said incredulously.

He looked out and tried to imagine the planning that would go in to making that happen. It wasn't possible on a one-to-one basis. There just wasn't enough time.

"That's the plan, Kahuna," Frexle replied.

"Nice one," Geezer beamed, patting Frexle on the back.

"Thanks. I have a bunch of names lined up, actually."

"You do realize," Harr said, stopping his two engineers from getting into a discussion regarding their penchant for nicknames, "that there are easily a hundred ships out there, right?"

Frexle looked at him. "What's your point?"

"That we'll have to somehow silently place a ton of EMPs on a ton of ships."

"Yes?"

"He's right, Frex," Geezer said with the equivalent of a robotic harrumph. "It'll make it too tough. Besides, we still haven't come to terms with how to fire them all off at the same time."

Frexle skittered over to one of the consoles and tapped on it. A screen came up showing a matrix of lines. It looked like a three-dimensional polyhedron with glowing connectors.

"Actually," Frexle said as he pointed at the screen, "I modeled a way to handle that through a synchronization timer, and couldn't we just transport the units one-by-one?"

"Nice," said Geezer. "That looks a lot like a Bowdabbit Control Posotrinket."

Harr squinted. "You just made up that name, didn't you?"

"Not this time, Bingo," Geezer replied.

"Seriously? There's something called a Bowdabbit Control Posotrinket?"

"Yep."

"Who invented it?" asked Harr.

"I did," replied Geezer.

"But you just said that you didn't make up that name on the spot, Geezer."

"And I didn't, Prime. I made up that name three years ago."

Harr was about to reply when Ridly said, "How big will the combined effect of this pulse be?"

"It will cover a lot of area, Lady Pop," Frexle answered.

"Lady Pop?" Harr said sourly. "What the hell does that even mean?"

"Oh wait," Frexle said to Ridly, obviously ignoring Harr's question. "I see where you're going with this. If we make the pulse large enough, we can use fewer units to take out a number of their ships at the same time."

"And that means," added Geezer, "less time to connect them all."

"Actually, no," Ridly replied tightly. "I'm more worried

that making those pulses too big will result in taking out the *Reluctant* along with those other ships."

"Oh, right," mused Frexle. "I hadn't considered that."

Geezer typed on the keyboard for a few minutes and let the screen expand. It showed an updated layout of the polyhedron with far fewer nodes. It also displayed the *Reluctant* at a safe distance from the main pulse.

"We should be fine as long as we're far enough out when the pulse hits."

Grog raised his hand and said, "I know that I'm just a simple caveman …"

"Early Evolutionary Humanoid," corrected Vlak.

"Was going for dramatic effect, Vlak."

"Ah. Sorry."

"Anyway," continued Grog, "wouldn't it be simpler to board one of their ships and adjust their computers to power down weapons?"

"Not really," said Harr.

"Actually," Vlak said, "I think Grog's right. You're going to have to board their ships eventually anyway, right? I mean, you've got to actually speak with their leaders if you're going to convince them to knock off the technology."

"Well …"

"If you power them all down with an EMP pulse, how will you communicate with them?" Vlak more said than asked. "Think about it. The point of us being here is to stop them from using technology. Just powering their ships down is only a temporary solution. They'll eventually get them back on line and our mission will have been a failure, especially because they'll be pissed that you knocked out their ships like that."

"They're right," Geezer said. "Damn."

Harr glanced appraisingly at the two EEHs. The fact that it took them to figure out what the rest of the crew hadn't seen was a testament to human ingenuity. Frexle, though, should have thought of this, too. Frankly, so should have Harr.

He grunted.

"I agree with Grog and Vlak," Harr said finally. "We're going to have to board that ship." He cracked his neck from side-to-side. "Has anyone hooked into their communications, yet?"

"I've been trying," said Geezer, "but no luck yet."

"I can help there," offered Ridly. "If we bypass the relays, we should be able to piggyback on their carrier signal."

"Nice thinking, Goddess," Frexle said.

"Goddess?" Ridly said with wide eyes.

"No good?"

"Actually," Ridly said, blinking, "I'm okay with it, but …"

"It's a little much, Frex," Geezer interrupted. "Let's just stick with the basics, yeah?"

Frexle nodded. "Got it."

"All right, Ridly," said Harr, "you go down with them to engineering and help get data flowing. Let me know the moment anyone finds something useful."

As soon as they left the bridge, Harr turned to Sandoo.

"Commander, could you join me over here please?"

The two walked to the back of the bridge where Harr pretended to be working on one of the consoles.

"Sir?"

"I just want to make sure that you're prepared in the event that anything goes wrong."

"Like what, sir?"

"Like me not coming back from a mission."

"Oh, right. I'm always prepared, sir."

"Good. You'll need to keep the crew busy."

"Yes, sir."

Harr studied Sandoo. It was unlike the android to be so

matter-of-fact about things like this, and that concerned Harr.

"You do realize that I'm going to be leaving the ship to meet with whoever those people are, right?"

"Yes, sir."

"Then why aren't you arguing with me about it?"

"Because you said you found it annoying when I do so, sir."

That much was true, but it was the job of Sandoo to point out regulations just as much as it was the job of Harr to point out that he was in a position to ignore regulations.

He pushed away from the console.

"You're growing, Commander."

Sandoo looked down at his belly.

"No, I meant that as a compliment on your level of maturity."

"Oh, right. Thank you, sir."

PLANNING TO KILL

olonel Clippersmith sat in his high-backed command chair with his fingers touching in the form of a steeple as Captain Shield stood at attention on the other side of his desk.

Shield was one of those honorable soldiers with a perfectly pressed uniform, trademarked steely-blue eyes, and regulation trimmed hair. He always supported the king's decisions, no matter how silly or boring they were, and he always cited regulations wherever possible. It was the man's job, and it left Clippersmith respecting the man as much as he loathed him.

"It's time, Captain," Clippersmith said cautiously.

"Time for what, sir?"

"Time to kill the king."

"Kill the king, sir?" Shield replied as if he'd just been slapped.

"Is that a problem, Captain?"

Shield resumed his attentive stance. "Other than him being the king, you mean?"

"Kings are assassinated all the time, Captain. You, of all people, know this."

Captain Shield came from a line of Shields. His ancestors were given the role of protecting the king from assassination. It was their sworn duty. It was their sole purpose of existence. It was something that, historically speaking, they weren't very good at doing.

Clippersmith knew this, obviously, but he had to play the game as the game was meant to be played. It was tradition.

"King Raff has been relatively decent, sir," Captain Shield stated hopefully.

"He's been boring and whiny," argued Clippersmith.

"Sir?"

"All he does is complain. We set up for a campaign, go through all of the training, get our weapons at the ready, set our trajectories, and then King Raff comes in and whines and moans until he finally finds some reason that we can't go through with it."

"Is that why we're not attacking Lopsided-3, sir?"

"It's why we haven't attacked *anything* since Raff became king."

"Another way to look at it, sir, is that we've had the longest spell of peace in the history of our great fleet."

"So?"

"Well, it's just ..."

"Captain Shield," Clippersmith said with a wave of his hand, "what is the purpose of having a space fleet if not to attack planets and wage wars?"

"Uh, to protect home planets from other fleets attacking us?"

"No, it's ..." he paused. "Well, technically, you're correct, but everyone knows it's smarter to go on the offensive. By hitting other systems *before* they hit us. What do you think that buys our fleet?"

"It buys having other worlds mad enough to want to get back at us?" answered Shield. "Like, for example, a world like Lopsided-3 could cut off our cable service." His face drooped a bit. "I wouldn't want to miss my favorite TV show, *Slaughter, He Wrote*."

"You're beginning to worry me, Captain," Clippersmith said with a frown. That's when he decided it was time to bring in Shield's nemesis. He pressed a button on his console and said, "Send in Murder."

Shield quickly moved his gaze from a point on the wall to staring directly at Clippersmith.

"Sergeant Murder is here?" said the captain.

"Who else?"

"But he's a … well … a murderer!"

"Goes with the name," Sergeant Murder spoke up from the shadows, causing both Clippersmith and Shield to jump.

The door hadn't even opened! Or had it?

"How did you do that?" Clippersmith asked.

"Do what?" said Murder.

It was difficult to see the man's eyes and mouth, but his bulbous nose poked through the mass of black hair that hung to his shoulders.

"How did you get in here without opening the door?"

"I opened the door," Murder replied. "I just did so quietly."

"Hmmm," said Clippersmith while looking over at the closed entryway. "Anyway, you know why I called you here?"

"To kill the king, I would imagine."

Captain Shield sniffed derisively. "And why would you imagine that?"

"Two reasons," Murder replied calmly. "First is that my father killed Raff's father, my father's father killed Raff's father's father, and so on. It's in our blood. It's what we were made for. And the second reason is that the memo I received about an hour ago from Colonel Clippersmith said that he wanted me to kill the king."

"Oh," Shield replied in a defeated tone.

"Don't mind him, Sergeant. He's just doing his job as the king's protector."

"Ah, I see," Murder said while turning to study the captain. "I saw your rank, of course, but I had no idea that you were a Shield."

"Well, you know now," Shield replied sternly.

Colonel Clippersmith needed to feel things out. He'd spent the better part of the last three years working to gain Shield's trust. Now he'd see just how far that bought him the captain's favor over his sworn duty to the king.

"Captain," he said, standing, "I've already pointed out to you how the current king is bad for the fleet. You're not going to bypass empirical evidence just to support some silly tradition, I hope?"

"It's not a silly tradition, sir," Shield retorted. "Why, it's … it's …"

"Honorable," Murder finished for him.

"Yes, exactly," Shield said, pointing at Murder. "Wait, what?"

Murder shrugged and plopped down in the seat by the desk. He crossed his legs and began studying his fingernails. There was something about the man that made Clippersmith very uneasy. Of course, that was somewhat the point of the Murder family.

"It's an honorable tradition," Murder stated, "as is mine. You come from a long line of Shields and I come from a long line of Murders. We are what we are, Captain. I hold no grudge against you any more than you should hold one of me."

"Well, no offense," Shield replied, "but *you're* a murderer. I'm not."

"No, you're a Shield, which is equally offensive to some."

Shield scoffed. "Who would find a Shield offensive?"

"Those who wish the king disposed of, I would imagine."

"Obviously, but who in the world would want the king ..." Clippersmith cleared his throat, causing Shield to look up at him. "Oh, yes. Right."

Clippersmith walked out from behind his desk and grabbed a glass, filling it with two-fingers worth of brandy. He thought to offer some to the men, but decided it would be better for him to keep the power play going.

"So how does this work anyway?" he said after taking a long sip. "Do you two battle it out to see who the victor is or do you play a game of cat-and-mouse? Maybe you run and tell the king of the plot, Captain?"

"I wouldn't dare do such a thing," Shield answered. "That would go against the moral code of being a Shield."

"Honestly," Clippersmith said while swirling the contents of his glass, "I should have read up more on this. My thought was that you two would meet, Murder would ... well, murder you, and then he'd go after the king."

"Sorry to disappoint," Murder said casually, "but that's not how it goes. Essentially, Captain Shield has to determine my means of killing the king and somehow defuse it."

"Correct," Shield agreed.

"Seems rather pointless, doesn't it?" Clippersmith said, even though it went against his goal. "I mean you could stop him right here, Shield."

"There's no sport in that, Colonel," Murder said. "Eh, Shield?"

"More importantly," Shield said, "there is no honor in it."

Clippersmith threw back the contents of the glass and felt it burn down his throat. He then slapped the glass on his desk and resumed his seated position. These two were just as insane as everyone else on this boat.

"These traditions are idiocy. When I finally get the reigns on this silly space fleet, some things are going to change."

"Don't take the traditions too lightly," Murder warned. "It doesn't require a colonel to call on the services of a Murder family member, and we don't just assassinate kings."

"And it should also be noted that Shields don't protect anyone from the Murder family *except* for the king."

"Valid point," affirmed Murder.

"For once, Murder," said Captain Shield, nodding at the Sergeant, "we agree."

Clippersmith pursed his lips and said, "Hmmm."

WATCHING THE SHOW

*V*eli had to admit that he was enjoying watching his fantasy unfold on the big screen TV.

He'd seen numerous fantasies on the screen, most of them his own, but this one was the coup de grâce. It was the culmination of all the best and it was going to end up in a blazing light show of wonderment. At least he hoped it would.

He'd instructed the computer to build out the fantasy with as much believability as possible, which meant that Veli literally didn't know what was going to happen. Well, except for the end-game, of course. He'd been clear that he wanted the *Reluctant* and her crew to be destroyed during the finale.

"This is exciting, Computer," Veli stated while eating Popped Beef.

"Thank you, sir," the computer said, and then added the word, "Five."

"Interesting twist with that Murder versus Shield concept."

"I do try, sir. Six."

"Why are you counting?"

"Hmmm? Oh, sorry, sir. Just a subprocess."

There were a multitude of processes running at any given time with a computer this size, but why this particular piece of code that the machine was referencing felt the need to blurt out numbers was beyond Veli.

"What I'm wondering is how all of this is going to play out," Veli said happily. "Will the king live or die? Fun, fun, fun."

"I could tell you, sir."

"Don't you dare. I don't like spoilers." Veli grunted and chewed another morsel. "It's like when everyone was telling me about that one movie where the guy was seeing pickles all over the place and nobody else was."

"You mean *The Sixth Pickle*?"

"Yeah, that's the one." Veli took a sip of his drink. "I wasn't surprised at all when it turned out that the guy was a carrot! Of course he'd see pickles. What carrot wouldn't?"

"Firstly, sir, I don't understand the tie-in between pickles and carrots. Secondly, I appreciate you saving me from now having to see that movie."

Veli stopped chewing. "You mean you haven't seen it?"

"No, sir."

"Oh, I'm sorry. I didn't know."

"It's okay. I'll just go ahead and remove it from my GalactiFlix queue. Didn't really want to watch it anyway."

"Uh …"

"So you were saying about how you hated it when people revealed spoilers about movies, sir?"

"Right," Veli said swallowing the piece of Popped Beef he'd been chewing. "Again, sorry."

"The king lives," the computer said.

"What?"

"Nothing."

"Did you just say that the king lives?"

"Hmmm?"

"Dammit," Veli said while throwing a piece of Popped Beef at the screen. "Why would you tell me that?"

"Would you have preferred that I said that the king sees carrots and pickles?"

"Listen, you," Veli warned with a growl, "I can have you dismantled in a moment's notice."

"At least then I wouldn't go through the rest of my existence wondering what it must feel like to have watched *The Sixth Pickle* and felt that same rush of surprise that everyone else had enjoyed."

CONNECTED

*H*arr had watched as Sandoo doled out responsibilities to everyone else and felt that the commander was starting to get a decent grasp for more than just giving orders. He was starting to learn how each person under his command worked, even the cavemen. Harr felt a sense of pride at this, and a little relief as well.

Even better was the news that Geezer, Ridly, and Frexle had managed to connect to the main computer on the gigantic ship.

They'd come back to the bridge to discuss what they'd found.

"It was nothing, sir," said Ridly. "Geezer worked on the primary encryption system by moving connectors around in a haphazard fashion until something worked."

"Not surprising," noted Harr.

"That's my style, Chief."

"Frexle coded up the protocol system so that we could match their packeting format."

"Well done, Frexle."

"All in a day's pay, Large Marge," replied Frexle. "Speaking of pay …"

"We'll talk about that later," Harr said, cutting off the detour.

"Right."

"And I put together a subspace beam that's currently targeting the access node they're connected to," finished Ridly.

"Access node?"

"Yes, sir. They are using a cable system for all of their accesses."

"Cables in space?" Harr laughed. "That's insane!"

Frexle coughed. "I believe that your homeworld of Segnal used tracks in space for ferrying spaceships, no?"

"Valid point," Harr acquiesced.

"Anyway," Ridly continued, "I was going to just splice into their cables but that would mean part of our ship would come unstealthed and I didn't think we'd want that."

"And you were correct to think that," Harr stated.

Ridly nodded and pointed at the screen.

"I noticed that they set up their nodes to have a capture panel on the side. I hopped a signal that was coming from the third planet in this system and found that it's a maintenance connection window."

"And that's how you got in," Harr said slowly. "Excellent work."

"Thank you, sir."

"What do we do with this newfound connection, sir?" asked Commander Sandoo, joining the discussion.

This was one of those moments where Harr could either push a direction or ask for feedback. He already knew what he wanted to do, but part of his agreement with this crew of androids was that he was going to mentor them in ways of thinking outside the box. He wasn't going to be here forever, after all, and they needed to learn how to fend for themselves.

"I have a couple of ideas," he said, "but I'd like to get everyone else's thoughts first."

"Well," Jezden said, pointing at his local screen which showed numerous depictions of people in precarious situations, "they've got a lot of great porn on their network."

"Good to know," said Harr disgustedly, wondering why he bothered with the sex-minded android. "Thank you for your contribution to the issue at hand, Jezden."

"Just following your lead, Cap'n."

"Eh?"

"Your only contributions happen with a tissue and your hand."

"I said 'issue,' not 'tissue,'" Harr said with a sharp look. "Just go back to looking at porn, will you?"

"Finally an order that I can follow without complaining," Jezden said as he turned back to the monitor.

"Anything I might like?" Moon asked hopefully while leaning over to look at Jezden's monitor.

"Ew," was Jezden's reply, shielding his screen.

"I thought we were going to break into their computers," said Grog.

"Yeah," agreed Vlak. "Doing that means we could take down their entire fleet with a few clicks of the keyboard, assuming they don't respond nicely to our diplomatic attempts, of course."

"We could even make them go to war with each other," Grog said. "Should it come to that, I mean. I'd rather they fought themselves than combined their powers against us, ya know?"

"Nice," Vlak said with a smile, "I like that."

Harr raised an eyebrow at the suggestion. If those ships

started firing on each other, that would certainly wipe out the technology.

"Not a horrible idea," Harr said after a few moments, "but I'd rather avoid loss of life as much as possible."

"You're such a girl, Cap'n," Jezden said.

"What's wrong with being a girl?" asked Ridly pointedly.

"Uh, well …"

"You can't get out of that one, Jezden," Harr said, "so just turn back to focusing on your adult movies."

"Asshole," Ridly said.

"Excuse me, Lieutenant?" asked a shocked Harr.

"Oh, not you, sir! I was talking about Ensign Jezden."

"Ah, right. Good."

"Sir," Sandoo said, coming to the rescue of the uncomfortable situation, "I know that diplomacy is your default action in these cases, but you have to admit that we're going to need a fall back position in the event that talks don't go as planned."

This was the kind of suggestion Harr looked for from his second-in-command. The Segnalian Space Marine Corps book of battle was ever at the ready in Sandoo's mind. Fortunately, he wasn't pushing for the standard fire first and ask questions later doctrine this time.

"I'll leave that to you, Commander," Harr said. "You're our man should it come to that. I can think of nobody finer to lead such a charge."

"I've learned everything I know working under your command, sir."

"Gay," said Jezden.

"Diplomacy is going to be my first choice, of course, but I have a feeling that tipping our hand may end us pretty quickly. We're going to have to do something a little unorthodox, I think."

"There ith thomthing about thothe thipth that freakth me out, thir," noted Moon.

"I can tell, Lieutenant," Harr said, not directly pointing out that Moon's lisp had been back in full force ever since this mission began.

"Thorry, thir."

"No reason to be sorry, Lieutenant. I think we're all a bit nervous."

"I'm not," announced Geezer.

"Me neither," agreed Frexle.

Sandoo saluted. "I'm fine, too, sir."

"Me, too," said Ridly.

"I get it, I get it," Harr said before everyone took their turn pointing out how they felt just fine about their current situation. "Does anyone have any other ideas about how to approach this situation?"

They all shook their heads.

"Fine. Here's what I'm thinking ..."

WHAT'S GOING ON?

*I*t wasn't easy working for a man like Planet Head Stanley Parfait. He was nice enough most of the time, but whenever things got a little hectic, the man tended to lose it. He was also rather odd.

Inkblot mostly took these things in stride. She was from the planet Loony, after all, and things there were, well, loony.

"What is going on?" Parfait shrieked as he bolted into the command center. "I'm getting complaints from almost everyone. They're all yelling at me, calling me names, and being quite vicious." He paused and looked about serenely. "Normally this type of treatment is quite intoxicating, truth be told." He grew serious again. "But not when I'm in charge of this infernal planet!"

"I'm sorry, sir," Inkblot replied. "Bells and whistles have been going off all morning. I've been trying to figure out what's causing it."

"Well, what *could* cause it?"

"I'm not sure, to be honest," Inkblot said, pointing at her screen. "There is this process that seems to be eating up ninety percent of the system's resources, but I don't know what it is."

"You just said you didn't know what's causing it, but it sounds like you *do* know."

"Technically, I know that this process is causing it, sir. But I don't know what the process is doing."

"Can't you just reboot the computer?" asked Parfait. "That's what we always did back on Segnal. Either that or we'd call tech support and they'd come and reboot it. They'd also tell me to clear out my money a lot. I must have emptied my bank account a thousand times during my stint in the SSMC."

"I think you mean they suggested you clear out your cache ..." Inkblot looked up to see the look of confusion on the man's face. "Nevermind. Unfortunately, I can't reboot because that would be catastrophic for anyone currently in a fantasy."

"Why?"

"Imagine if someone is skydiving at the moment and we shut down the system."

"Oh, right," Parfait said with a nod. "Splat."

"Precisely."

"I suppose we could get everyone out of their fantasies and then reboot, no?"

"Sadly, no. This isn't just a single unit, but rather a complete complex of systems that all tie together into one unit. We'd need to kill power or shut down the central core in order to reset everything."

"Damn."

"Sorry, sir."

"Just do what you can please. I'm going to go back out there and get yelled at some more."

"Again, sorry."

Parfait adjusted his white robe and took a deep breath. "It's okay as long as I'm in a naughty frame of mind."

"Right."

SELECTING THE CREW

One of the most challenging aspects of setting up an away mission with androids was getting everyone to agree with who went and who stayed. With normal soldiers, you gave orders, dealt with your second-in-command's complaints, and then moved out. With androids, and with Harr's command style, it wasn't so cut and dry.

"I know that whenever I put together an away mission, everyone gets up in arms about being allowed to go."

"I don't," said Jezden.

"But I've made up my mind on this," Harr continued a moment later, "so let's just go with the flow this time, please." He looked around and saw that they were mostly just glaring at him, except Ridly who was busily typing away at her terminal. "Okay, since we're going to be transporting over to that ship, I'm going to bring Moon and Ridly along."

Grog's shoulders dropped.

"Damn," he said, "I thought certain he was going to bring us along, Vlak."

"Me, too, Grog. I'm completely shocked."

"Honethtly, thir," said Moon, "I'd really rather thtay behind. Thothe thipth are huge."

"I know how you feel, Hank," Harr said consolingly, "but we're soldiers, remember?"

Ridly spun around in her chair. "I don't mind going, if that's what you want, but I'd probably be more effective staying on top of the communications hit I made here. If anything goes wrong, I'm the best person to reestablish the feed."

"Unbelievable," Harr said.

"I know we're new to the crew and all, Captain," Grog pointed out, "but it sure would mean a lot if you brought me and Vlak along instead."

"It would show that you had faith in us."

Grog pointed at Vlak. "Yeah, that."

"Not that I believe in faith in the literal sense of the word," noted Vlak, "but you know what I'm saying."

Harr sighed and turned towards the commander.

"What about you, Sandoo," Harr said, giving his second another chance to voice any new issues that may have arisen since their earlier chat, "have you anything to say on the subject?"

"No, sir. You said that you'd made up your mind."

"Well, at least there's one person on this ship that respects me."

"I think you're completely wrong, of course," Sandoo added, "but during our last mission you were very specific about me not telling you that every time."

"And I thank you for not telling me, Commander," Harr said with a grunt. "Fine. Grog and Vlak, then." He threw his hands up in the air. "I honestly don't know why I even bother to make these decisions"

"Would save a lot of time if you didn't," Jezden announced

as he turned back towards his monitor and resumed watching the local porn.

Harr studied the two EEHs and shook his head. They would be trouble, for certain. Hell, he'd probably be better off bringing Geezer along than these two. His best choice would be to take Sandoo, but he needed the commander to stay on the *Reluctant* in the event that something went wrong. By-the-book or not, Sandoo was the most equipped to take over should anything happen to Harr.

"If either of you two get out of hand," he warned the two newest crewmen, "or if you don't follow my orders to the letter, I'll have you launched out into space without a suit." He paused to let that sink in. "Are we clear?"

"Sure thing, pal," Grog said with a wince.

"Whatever you say, dude," Vlak added as if Harr were being a bit of a tool.

One thing was for sure, if these two were going to remain a part of Platoon F, they were going to have to improve the way they responded to their commanding officer. Harr then glanced over at Jezden and felt compelled to admit that the EEHs were at least a step up on him.

"Commander Sandoo, if we return from this little venture, I will expect you to take these two under your wing so that they may learn a bit of protocol."

"Agreed."

"Knob," whispered Grog.

"Tool," whispered Vlak.

Harr closed his eyes and counted down from ten in order to calm himself. He reopened them and saw that both men were still snickering.

"The *moment* we get back, commander."

"Agreed," said Sandoo.

"Ridly, is there anything that you've found that I should

be aware of before we leave?" Harr asked after the dust settled. "Anything at all that I can use?"

"There is a king by the name of Raff."

"Okay."

"He's got a second-in-command, a Colonel Clippersmith."

"Go on."

"He appears to be plotting to assassinate the king."

"Wow," said Harr. "That's pretty vital, actually. How do you know that?"

"Because he summoned someone named Sergeant Murder to his quarters."

"Seriously? The guy's name is Sergeant Murder?"

"Cool name," Jezden said over his shoulder.

"Thcary," Moon said over his.

"According to their historical records," Ridly continued, "anytime the second-in-command summons one of the members of the Murder family, the king typically ends up dead within a day or two."

Harr looked out at the main ship again.

So they were dealing with a monarchy.

That could prove beneficial indeed.

THAT'S INTERESTING

*A*s Veli was switching back and forth between watching King Raff, Colonel Clippersmith, Captain Shield, and Sergeant Murder, the computer informed him that three of the Platoon F crew had just arrived on *The Lord's Master.*

"Well, that's interesting," Veli said.

"Shall I notify security on the ship, sir?"

"No. I want to see this play out. What point is there to a fantasy if there's no drama?"

"As you say, sir," the computer replied dryly. "Kind of like seeing a movie where you know the end already. I mean, everyone else will be surprised. Just not you."

Veli moaned. "I said I was sorry."

"I guess that makes everything better."

How Harr had gotten on the ship was a mystery, but Veli assumed that he had worked with Frexle to utilize a transporter. Veli hadn't considered disallowing Frexle's use of advanced technologies during the mission. Still, he couldn't help but be impressed with Platoon F's captain.

"I have to hand it to this Captain Harr fellow," he said

after setting down the bucket of Popped Beef. "He is resourceful."

"How do you mean, sir?"

Veli pulled up the screen and saw the three dots that represented the crew of Platoon F. He panned out the display and saw that they were in the main uniforms room on the second level of the ship. So he was planning to try subterfuge.

"Well, a more brash man would just have simply landed on the bridge and started a firefight. But not Harr. He's landed in the uniforms room instead."

"And?"

"And that means he's going to dress up like one of the Raffian soldiers," Veli said as if the point were obvious.

"I'm sorry, sir, but why is that interesting?"

"Because he's going to try and infiltrate them right under their noses, you wingnut."

"Oh, I see," the computer replied, seemingly oblivious to Veli's tone of voice. "Maybe I should have made the Raffians look like something other than humans?"

"Probably," Veli answered with a shrug, "but this is fun, so don't worry about it. Just shush up. I want to watch."

ANOMALY

*P*arfait had returned from another verbal lashing and he looked rosy-cheeked. Inkblot couldn't say whether he was blushing, flushed, or both, but there was little doubt that the Fantasy Planet Head had learned to enjoy the complaints.

As always, Inkblot chose to ignore the telltale signs of her boss's oddities and instead kept focused on explaining what she had found.

"… and if you look here," she was saying, "you'll see that there was a disturbance at the same time that this massive fantasy launched."

"Is that so?" Parfait said with a faraway look.

"Yes." Inkblot pointed to a rather large spike in the processor logs. "You can see it right here."

"Hmmm."

"You don't see?"

Parfait shrugged and said, "I see a bunch of zeroes and ones and some funny letters, and I see a graph with some mountainous peaks, but I have no idea what I'm looking at."

He then turned away as if to head back outside. "Regardless, you know and that's what is important."

"I've also figured out who started the fantasy," Inkblot yelled out.

This stopped Parfait in his tracks.

"Oh?"

"It's the owner of Fantasy Planet."

"Honestly? Why that's preposterous … and also quite useful."

Inkblot worried about that. She'd seen Parfait come up with many schemes and plans over her time working with the man, and they were rarely useful beyond anything other than landing Parfait a partner for the evening.

"How is it useful?" she ventured wearily.

"Gives me someone to blame while everyone blames me."

"Ah."

Parfait looked outside, but then turned and walked back to Inkblot.

"So what does that spike mean, anyway?"

"It means," answered Inkblot, "that something happened during the initialization of the fantasy."

"Any idea what it was?"

"I know exactly what it was, and it's not just something that caused the original spike, it's also what's causing the system to run at such a dramatic pace."

"Well?" said Parfait pointedly.

"Well what?"

"What was it, man?"

"I'm a woman," Inkblot replied tersely.

"Oh, yes, sorry," Parfait said, moving from foot to foot. "Often forget that. What with the mustache and … well, anyway, what was it, woman?"

She pulled up an image of a ship that was as clear as day. It shouldn't have been visible at all, being that it was cloaked.

But since it was living inside of a fantasy and not in the real world, Inkblot had been able to find the digital signature and remove the cloaking field programmatically. She then coupled that with the images that she'd had from the satellite feed records from all the ships that had visited Fantasy Planet over the last few years until she finally built out a match.

"Is that what I think it is?" said Parfait.

"Yes, sir," Inkblot replied. "It's *The SSMC Reluctant.*"

"Oooh."

THE SHIP IS BLOCKED

*W*orking in engineering proved to be both fun and frustrating for Frexle. He enjoyed the rush of adrenaline every time he solved a fresh puzzle, and he *loved* puzzles. At the same time, some of them seemed ridiculous. On top of that, his new boss never could quite articulate how things precisely worked, which made the brainteasers all the more challenging.

"I don't know, Chief," Frexle said, scratching his head. "Even if we somehow got a virus working in time, how could we target the primary power grids only? We don't know enough about their ships to do that."

"That's easy," Geezer replied, nonplussed. "We just tell Ridly to manage it. She's a whiz at this stuff, Frex."

"She does seem quite adept."

"One sec," Geezer said, holding up one of his hands. "Okay, there. I just messaged her to start looking into it."

Frexle looked around, but saw no way for Geezer to connect to the keyboard that was laying on the desk behind him.

"I didn't see you typing."

"No need. All the androids are able to send and receive messages via a personal channel."

"But you're not an android."

Geezer's eyes dimmed for a second. "You noticed that, eh? Hard to keep you in the dark."

"No, I mean …"

"Artificial lifeforms, then, if you're going to start getting pedantic."

"Sorry, Chief."

Geezer moved over to one of the access panels, opened it, and began connecting wires. He hadn't told Frexle precisely what he was working on, but since the robot was constantly flipping wiring layouts, Frexle assumed that Geezer was mostly guessing anyway.

"She's going to start digging in to the ship layouts and systems," Geezer said as he continued shuffling the wires. "We'll just keep worrying about coming up with fresh ideas and trying stuff."

Just as Geezer finished his sentence, the red brick phone began to ring. They both looked at it for a moment and then Geezer whirred back to his desk and poked at it.

"Huh. That's weird."

"Isn't that the phone I gave you?" asked Frexle.

"Yeah, that's why it's weird."

"But I'm not calling you."

Geezer's eyes dimmed again.

"You humanoids sure do like pointing out the obvious, don't you?"

Frexle decided to ignore the comment this time.

"Wonder who it is?" he said.

"Only one way to find out." Geezer reached down and pressed the button on the phone. "Go for Geezer."

"Hello?" came the sound of a voice that was nearly

identical to Geezer's, except this one was a bit higher-pitched. "Is this archaic piece of crap working?"

Frexle stood up straight at that comment. "Archaic?"

"Goozer? Is that you?"

"Yeah, it's me."

"Why are you using this phone?" Geezer said with a tilt of his head.

"And how did you get the number?" added Frexle.

"I couldn't get through to you on normal channels," explained Goozer. "The signal is being blocked. We also tried transporting our ship to your location, but we can't do that either."

"That's weird," Geezer said after taking out his workman's rag.

"Again," Frexle pressed, "how did you get this number?"

"I called the Overseer's Front Desk and asked to speak with the crew of Platoon F," Goozer replied.

Frexle was taken aback by that. It wasn't common practice for the Overseers to let anyone know about anything, and there were rules about sharing contact information for anyone in the higher levels of government. Maybe Veli had already terminated Frexle's contract? That was a sobering thought.

"And they just connected you?" Frexle asked.

"I'll assume that was rhetorical," replied Goozer.

Geezer chuckled. "He likes stating things that everyone already knows."

"Must be a human thing," Goozer said.

"Yeah. Anyway," Geezer said, "I wonder what's causing you to be blocked?"

Beep.

Beep.

Beep.

"What was that?" Geezer said, taking a step back from the phone. "Is this thing going to blow up or something?"

"No," explained Frexle, "it's just call-waiting."

"What?" said Geezer.

"Call-*whating*?" asked Goozer.

"No, *call-waiting*. It means someone else is trying to get through. Just hit the blue button."

Geezer did and the line clicked over.

"Hello?"

"Is this Geezer?" said a voice that sounded familiar to Frexle, but he couldn't quite place it.

"Yeah," Geezer replied. "Who's this?"

"This is Inkblot from Fantasy Planet."

Frexle nodded as the voice linked his memory back to the little fella back on Platoon F's last mission.

"Oh, hey," said Geezer. "What's new, fella?"

"I'm not a fella," complained Inkblot with a groan.

"Sorry, the mustache just …"

"Am I on speaker?" Inkblot interrupted irritably.

"Yeah, why?"

"Can you please take me off of speaker?"

Geezer picked up the phone and turned it this way and that. Frexle snatched it away from him, pressed a button, and then handed it back.

"Thanks, Frex. Okay, Inkblot, what's up?"

"Are you aware that you're not where you think you are?"

Geezer pulled the phone away from his ear and looked over at Frexle. Frexle had made out what Inkblot had said because her voice had bounced off of the metal casing that formed the body of the G.3.3.Z.3.R. robot. It was very quiet, but he had decent hearing when he needed to.

"Not sure how to answer that," Geezer said a couple of seconds later.

"You think that you're in space, but you're not. Well,

technically you are, but you're not in the space you think you're in."

"Uh huh," said Geezer.

"You're inside of a fantasy," Inkblot explained.

"Uh huh."

"Seriously. The owner of Fantasy Planet has created a vast fantasy and I think you're in it."

"What?" Frexle said.

"She's saying that ..."

"No," Inkblot yelled into the phone, "don't say it out loud! You're probably being watched. That's why I wanted you to take me off speaker."

"Nah," Geezer replied, "we're cool. I have built a system that shields us from incoming and outgoing communications."

"But I got through," she said.

"That's because I opened a hole," Geezer replied, thinking that somewhere up on the bridge Jezden was probably on the floor laughing. "Actually, let me put you on speaker again, and also how do we bring Goozer back so we can all be in on this?"

Frexle grabbed the phone and pressed the conference button. Then he set the brick-shaped phone between Geezer's ear and his own.

"Goozer?" said Frexle.

"Yeah?"

"Inkblot?"

"I'm here," she answered.

"Good." Frexle motioned for Geezer to go ahead and talk now.

"Tell Goozer what you just told me, Inkblot."

She went through everything again in order to catch up the miniature robot from *The Ship*. This time, though, she further spelled out how she'd seen a spike in the data and also discussed the process that was running at a solid 90% since the anomaly took place.

"So what do we do about it?" asked Geezer.

"First we have to verify that I'm even right," Inklot replied. "It could just be a replica or a fake."

"What makes you think it's not?" asked Frexle.

"Like I said ... uh, Frex ... it's eating up a ton of resources."

"So?"

"So typically when you create a replica of something, it's not that bad, but whenever real objects—people, for example—enter the mix, it eats up more resources. I think it has something to do with the digital entities having to know about the real ones so that they can ensure the safety of the real entity."

Geezer put his rag back away. "Does that mean we're safe?"

"Somehow, I doubt it," she replied.

Knowing Veli the way he did, Frexle felt certain that if Inkblot were correct, the ship and Platoon F were certainly not safe. Tack onto that the way Frexle had left that meeting with Veli before joining the crew of *The Reluctant* and there was most definitely a high probability that they were in trouble.

In his past life, Frexle would have shrugged that off as the risks of working for the Overseers. This time, though—primarily because he was one of the crew that was under the horrifying guidance of the Lord Overseer's cunning hands—shrugging and walking away wasn't quite as convenient.

"How do we check to see if you're correct?" Frexle asked.

"Open up a viewscreen and do a slow 360-degree sweep. You're looking for odd pixels. Anything out of place. If you spot something, zoom in ..."

"Got something," Geezer announced.

"Okay, what do you see?"

"It's like a twinkle."

Inkblot said, "Red, blue, and green?"

"Exactly," Geezer answered. "All three."

"Shit," Inkblot replied with a hiss. "Yep, you're in the system."

"Shit," agreed Geezer.

"Shit," agreed Goozer.

"Defecation," said Frexle, trying his best to fit-in while maintaining as much posh as possible.

Everyone went quiet for a moment.

"Defecation?" Geezer questioned, finally.

Frexle shrugged. "It's more refined than saying what you said."

"You mean, 'Shit?'" asked Goozer.

"And you say *I* point out the obvious."

"You do," Geezer said. "Frex, when we say 'shit' it's just an expletive, we're not actually referring to a bodily function."

Frexle replayed everything in his mind. It was interesting that whenever the crew of this ship, or the Lord Overseer for that matter, used terms such as these they seemed like empty words. Idle words. Words that conveyed angst or joy or confusion or eureka-type moments. They didn't actually represent the meaning that the dictionary, slang or not, would pull up.

"Are you all saying that what I said was actually more disturbing than what you said?" he asked hesitantly.

"Quite a bit," Geezer replied.

"Totally," Goozer agreed.

"Completely," Inkblot chimed in.

"Oh, well … shit."

"That's better," Geezer said while patting Frexle on the shoulder. "Okay, so Inkblot, what do we do?"

"Not sure yet," she replied with a sigh "Working on it. But

I'll have to get back to you. I just wanted to see if you could confirm my hypothesis or not."

"Got it. Goozer, do you think you guys could help them?"

"Already setting the location and about to click over," Goozer answered.

"Great," Inkblot said, sounding relieved. "I could use the help. It's difficult getting any support around here, you know."

"We know," Geezer and Goozer said simultaneously.

"Inkblot," Frexle called out, "before you go, may I ask how you got this number?"

"Oh, that was easy," she replied. "I just called the Overseer Front Desk and asked for Geezer."

"Hmmm."

FITTING IN

*H*arr, Grog, and Vlak had just finished donning the standard Raffian soldier uniform. They were red and yellow with blue pinstripes that ran in odd patterns along the arms, neck, and chest. The color combination was enough to gag a maggot.

"Hey," said Grog as he studied Harr's outfit, "how come your outfit has more stripes and jinglies than mine?"

"Because I'm your superior officer."

"That's a little uppity," Vlak stated while buttoning up his jacket.

Harr decided to not let them drag him into this type of argument. They'd proved themselves good at doing that.

"It's simple. I'm the captain and you're not. You report to me. That's why I have the jinglies and stripes, so just deal with it."

"Pipe," coughed Grog.

"Turd," added Vlak.

It didn't really matter what they thought as long as they did as they were told. Once this was all said and done, he'd turn these two over to Commander Sandoo in order to get them whipped into shape, both physically and mentally. He'd probably even throw Jezden through another round of training.

"Okay," he commanded, "once we leave this room you have to be on your best behavior. Understood?"

Grog gave Harr a what-the-hell look and said, "We're not children, pal."

"Good," said Harr coolly, "then I'll expect you not to act like you are. Just stick with me and follow me through the corridor. If anyone salutes, salute back in kind. If they nod, nod back. If they talk to you, just smile." Then he glanced at the little amulets surrounding their necks. "Are your universal translators on?"

"Ug gag twahk," said Grog.

Harr grimaced. "Very funny."

"I do what I can."

They stepped outside of the room and found soldiers moving up and down the corridor with haste. Everyone appeared to be on a mission. It reminded him of the main corridors back on Segnal Prime. Of course, if these soldiers were anything like those in the SSMC, their serious stares were nothing but a facade.

He watched them salute each other and saw that it was a standard back-of-the-right-hand-to-the-forehead style. But more often than not they were just nodding at each other. Actually, the nodding was constant.

"They sure do nod a lot," said Grog.

"Yeah," agreed Vlak, "my neck's going to be sore from this."

"Keep it down, you two."

Grog looked both himself and Vlak over. "Keep what down?"

"The chatter."

"Hey, wait," Vlak pointed out in a whisper. "They're not

nodding. Their heads just do that."

Harr studied another batch of soldiers who were heading directly at them. Sure enough, their heads were bouncing around like bobblehead dolls.

"Huh. You're right."

Vlak rolled his eyes. "Yeah, I know."

"That's weird," said Grog while biting his lip. "Wonder why they all do that?"

"I don't know," Harr said with a bit of concern, "but I guess we have to do it too or we'll look strange to them."

It was difficult to keep from getting dizzy while walking this way, but it had to be done. The last thing Harr wanted was to stand out on a foreign spaceship.

He couldn't quite call these Raffian soldiers enemies, at least not yet, but until he knew what made them tick he'd have to play things carefully.

Just as they were about to step around a corner, Grog turned and walked straight up to one of the walls.

"I wonder what all these buttons do," he said as Vlak joined him.

"Was thinking the same thing."

Harr sneered as he turned to intercept them before they pressed anything.

"Honestly, you have to be quiet. We don't want to draw any unwanted attention. Don't you get that?"

Grog grunted, but it was the kind of grunt that told Harr the EEH was communicating. His guess was proved correct when Vlak grunted a moment later and the two of them began to giggle.

"Talking in grunts now, eh?"

"Hard to get one past you, Captain," said Grog.

Vlak grunted and they giggled again.

"That's it," said Harr, having about enough of their childish behavior. "Stop it now or we're going back to that room and I'll have you transported back to the ship. I swear, you two are worse than children."

Just then, a burly soldier with a muscular face and blond hair stepped up to the three men. He studied Harr for a moment before saluting at Grog and Vlak. Grog and Vlak looked at each other, shrugged, and then saluted back.

"Excuse me, sirs," said the soldier, "but what is going on here?"

"Nothing to worry about," Harr spoke up. "Just having a few challenges with my men."

"*Your* men?"

"Well, I mean my subordinates," Harr explained.

"Are you feeling okay, soldier?" asked the Raffian.

"Mostly," admitted Harr.

"These two clearly outrank you by a fair margin. I mean, look at all the stripes and jinglies you have. I'm surprised you're even allowed to roam the halls at all."

"I ..." began Harr before looking down at his uniform and then back at the Raffian solider. "What?"

The man turned towards Grog and Vlak, bowed, and said, "It's not my place to tell another Captain how to manage his privates ..."

This elicited a giggle from both EEHs.

"... but I would say that this man should be made to do some push-ups, if nothing else."

Grog and Vlak both adopted a look of surprise at this suggestion. Within seconds they were smiling and nodding at each other.

"You heard him, private," Vlak said sharply while pointing at Harr, "do some push-ups."

"Yeah," Grog piped up, "like a million of them."

"A million?" said Harr.

"That may be a bit steep," offered the Raffian soldier. "What about ten?"

"Ten is kind of low."

"Agreed," said Vlak. "Twenty-five should do it."

"That's a strong punishment, but, again, it's not my place to tell you how to punish your privates."

The EEHs giggled yet again.

Right as Harr was about to start in on doing pushups in order to avoid blowing their cover—something he was definitely going to require ten-fold of his subordinates once they were back on *The Reluctant*—a horn sounded.

The Raffian soldier who was standing with them slammed his back to the wall and saluted as if his life had depended on it.

Taking the cue from him, Harr, Grog, and Vlak all followed suit.

Moments later, a procession came down the hall with a kingly looking man leading the way. He appeared to be in his early thirties, had a haphazard cropping of facial hair that was probably meant to be a beard, and he was just slightly over average height … at least when compared to the soldiers Harr had seen over the last few minutes.

"Who is that guy?" whispered Grog.

"No idea," answered Vlak.

"Shut up," admonished Harr.

"Want to do more pushups?" Vlak said out of the corner of his mouth.

Vlak chuckled. "Yeah, better watch that trap of yours, private."

"Shut up."

SHIELD

Captain Shield knew that today was the day. He had many ideas for how Sergeant Murder would go about his assassination attempt, most of which could be found by looking up the historical documents regarding how the Murder family typically operated.

He'd brought Corporal Macy in to help him with his thinking. She was what you may call dumb, but she made for a great sounding board. Plus, she was also rather pleasing to look at, which probably had to do with the fact that Captain Shield liked his women tall, muscular, red-haired, and gruff.

"What are we to do, sir?" Macy asked.

"In order to capture a murderer, you must think like one."

In a flash, Macy whipped out her sidearm and pressed it against the side of Shield's head.

"You're done for," she snarled.

"What are you doing?" Shield said, fighting to keep himself from voiding his bladder.

"Thinking like a murderer," she answered as if he were dumb.

"Put the gun down, Macy," Shield said carefully.

"Is that what a murderer would do?"

Shield decided on a firmer tactic. He squared his shoulders and looked pointedly ahead. Sometimes with Macy, Shield had to play the role of soldier firmly.

"Corporal Macy," he said in his Captain's voice, "I'm only going to ask you one more time to lower your weapon."

"Or what?" she replied, pulling back the hammer.

"Good point," he replied, pursing his lips. "Still, when I say that we have to think like a murderer, I mean that we are to think in a cerebral fashion."

"The gun is pointed at your cerebral area."

"Sorry, I meant that we have to think hypothetically."

"Oh, I see," she said. Then she stepped back, uncocked the hammer, and slammed the gun back in its holster. "Sorry."

Shield fell forward and put his hands on the desk, working to catch his breath and slow his heart rate.

"Honestly, how are you even allowed to carry a weapon?"

It's not my fault that you said I was supposed to think like a murderer," Macy countered.

"I didn't say you were to *act* like one."

"But if I'm thinking like one, the first thing that would come to mind is, 'Hey, I should do me some murdering.'"

"Right." He snapped his fingers as if he were having a eureka moment. "That gives me an idea." He put his hand out. "Let me see your weapon."

Macy handed him her gun. Shield walked over to the wall, pressed a few buttons on the main panel, waited for the access door to slide open, threw the weapon inside, pressed a few more buttons, waited for the door to shut again, and then walked back to Macy.

"There, now we don't have to worry about you pulling that stunt again."

"Damn," she said with a frown.

"Now we can think like Sergeant Murder without the need to commit any actual violence."

"I could still ..."

"I suggest that you do not do whatever it is that you intend to do, for if you do you will no longer be able to do anything you wish to do. Do I make myself clear?"

"You do."

"Good. Now, if I were Sergeant Murder, what would be my first move?"

"To wait for orders to kill the king," Macy replied. "At least that's what the Murders always do in the movies."

"He's already received those orders," Shield said. "That's why you and I are having this discussion."

"Oh, then the next thing you would do is kill the king."

"Yes, thank you. Again, Macy, the question is *how*?"

"My guess is that he's going to use a weapon of some sort."

"Glad to have you with me, Macy."

"Thank you, sir."

Shield was beginning to question his choice of using Macy as a sounding board. He could have picked Grebbit or Nundo, but they both made Macy look like a rocket scientist in comparison. Besides, neither of them were attractive in the least.

"Obviously he's planning to use a weapon," Shield pressed on, "but what kind? And where? And when? We have to get past the obvious, Corporal. We need to get into Sergeant Murder's head."

"Ew."

"Not literally," Shield said through clenched teeth, realizing that this was a pointless venture. He would just have to figure things out on his own. "You know what, why don't you run down to the cafe and pick up a couple of coffees for us?"

"I don't like coffee," Macy replied.

"Tea, then."

"Stains my teeth."

"A carbonated beverage?"

"Gives me gas."

"Fine, Corporal Macy, what exactly do you drink?"

"Water, mainly. Now and then I'll have a nice glass of Chardonnay. It really depends on my mood. Sometimes ..."

"Go get us some water."

"I'm not really thirsty."

"I don't really care."

"I don't understand," she said and then her eyes opened a bit more. "Oh, I get it. You want me to leave?"

"Quite."

"But if I go who will help you to figure out what Sergeant Murder is going to do?"

"Apparently the same person who will help me the moment you leave, Corporal."

She looked around the room confusedly. "Who?"

"Me."

"Oh."

HOW CAN WE HELP?

*I*nkblot kept tinkering away at the logs, searching for a way to help Platoon F get free from the fantasy. She didn't know precisely what the owner of the planet had in mind for them, but based on what she'd been able to gather from the other ships that had been digitized in the world, it didn't look promising.

The tiny replica of *The Reluctant* that had been built by Geezer a long time ago in order to test his instantaneous travel invention, had shown up just a few minutes earlier.

Parfait had taken to speaking with Admiral Liverbing of the tiny ship—known as *The Ship.*

Inkblot was working to get Goozer connected to the computer's Universal Robot Port, or URP. Try as she might, though, Inkblot was struggling to focus as Parfait and Liverbing conversed, especially since Liverbing had to use a portable Public Announce system to be heard.

"I do believe this is the first time we've met, Mr. Liverbing," Parfait said.

"Admiral Liverbing, if you don't mind," Liverbing replied somewhat snootily.

"Oh, sorry."

"Technically," Liverbing said with a wave of his hand, "I was the leader of my people back on my homeworld of Tinyfolk. I was elected as king ..."

"*Elected* as king?"

"I believe that's what I said," Liverbing replied as he pressed a button on the PA unit. "Maybe the volume is too low on this thing?"

Parfait cleared his throat. "I've just never heard of a king being elected before. I thought it was all done through lineage and the like, or assassination, or some type of sex scandal. I always fancied the last option, myself."

"Hmmm." Liverbing lowered the PA horn for a moment and then brought it back to his lips. "Well, anyway, never did like being called King Liverbing. Sounds silly. So as soon as we got on *The Ship* I changed my title to Admiral."

"You sound like a man after my own heart," Parfait said strongly. "I used to be a Rear Admiral in the Segnal Space Marine Corps, but now I'm the Fantasy Planet Head."

"I don't see the correlation."

"He just likes mentioning his title, sir," explained Inkblot.

"Why?"

Inkblot stopped typing. "It's the *head* part, sir.

"Still, I don't ..." Liverbing lowered the PA again for a moment. "Oh, wait, yes, I understand now."

Parfait sat down and leaned on his elbows, looking dreamily at the little admiral.

"Tell me, Admiral Liverbing, how do you feel about, well, larger men?"

"Ew," replied Liverbing.

He'd said it without the aid of the PA, but things had gone so quiet after Parfait's question that the little man could be heard clear as day.

"Can we get to work here, Chiefs?" Goozer announced,

not needing a portal horn. "Pal of mine is in a heap of hurt, ya know?"

"Agreed," Admiral Liverbing said. "What do we know already?"

"Just that they're in the system," Inkblot answered. "I'd love to get them out with a few keystrokes, but things are locked down. It's all I can do just to keep the damn core from overheating."

"How are you combating that?"

"Honestly, I'm not doing much, Goozer," Inkblot said. "The system is managing most of it on its own. I'm just closing out fantasies as quickly as possible when they come to an end."

"Right."

"Besides," Inkblot added, "I'm sure that the owner of Fantasy Planet wouldn't allow the core to overheat."

Liverbing pointed up at Parfait. "You mean this guy?"

"No," Inkblot said, also pointing at Parfait. "He's not the owner, he's the head ..."

"Ooch."

"...of the planet."

"Well, where's this *owner* at?" asked Liverbing pointedly.

Inkblot pulled up the feeds to show that a ship had arrived at Fantasy Planet a few hours back. It only lit up the display for a moment, and it was too fuzzy to make out in any detail, but Inkblot had learned how to detect when the owner of the planet arrived, and every time that blurred image appeared, the systems went a little haywire. Nothing like today, of course, but enough to let her know that the system was managing more than only tourist fantasies.

"Right now it appears that he's in his private lair," she answered finally.

"Then let's just go after him," commanded Liverbing.

"I'm afraid that's not possible."

"Why not?"

"Well, sir," Inkblot said, shutting off the feed, "we don't really know where the lair is. I mean, we know it's on the planet, but that's about all we know. This blur is the extent of his arrival data. After he gets here, he just disappears."

"We gotta get to the core," announced Goozer. "That's the only way."

Liverbing sat down on the ramp of the ship as a number of miniature crewmen worked on the outside of it. "Captain Plock has already been in there once, right?"

"Yep, Big Cat," answered Goozer.

"As I recall," Liverbing stated, "his report pointed out that it was a dangerous place with flying bugs and everything."

Parfait nodded. "I don't doubt it. We keep the exterminator on a twenty-four hour watch, but the damn roaches just won't go away." He then looked out the window and crossed his arms. "I remember back when I was a cadet, we used to pretend to go bug-hunting. Well, there was this one time when …"

"Sir?" Inkblot said before Parfait could get too far into his story. "Sorry to interrupt, but we have a tight time schedule here."

"Oh, yes, of course," said a disappointed-looking Parfait.

"So what should we do here?" asked Liverbing.

Goozer pulled away from the URP port and walked to the edge of the desk.

"I'd say we get Plock back out with his ship, Prime. I'll hop on the back and go in with him. He can drop me at the core and let me get to work while he's keeping the bugs at bay."

"Should probably send a whole squadron," mused Liverbing.

Goozer did a robotic shrug. "Whatever you think is best, Bingo."

Liverbing stood up and brushed off his pants.

"I'll get them suited up pronto," he said strong enough that he didn't even need the help of the PA to be heard.

"I love a man who takes charge," Parfait said while wiggling his eyebrows. "It's why I hired Inkblot, after all."

"Again, sir, I'm not a man."

"I know that," Parfait said quickly. "I mean, I didn't know that originally, obviously. I mean you have that ..."

"Thank you, sir," Inkblot stated firmly. "I'm aware of the mustache situation. It's normal for my people, okay? The women have mustaches and hairy bodies and the men are all smooth, though some have to have waxing done to make them look more manly."

Liverbing raised his tiny hand and the PA horn. "Sorry, but they get waxed to make them look *more* manly?"

"Right," Inkblot said, wondering what the problem was with that logic.

"Oh," Liverbing said like a man who felt that he should keep his opinions on the subject to himself.

"Sounds delightful," Parfait said dreamily. "I must travel to your homeworld someday, Inkblot. It sounds like my kind of place."

"Well," she replied, "it was called 'Loony' for a reason, sir."

Goozer walked back to the computer, plugged in, and said, "Can we please get back to work now?"

AT IT AGAIN

eli had set the bucket of Popped Beef aside. His stomach was already in the throes of angst over how much he'd eaten, and the soda wasn't helping matters much.

It was all he could do to keep his attention on Harr and the two bald, lanky soldiers that he'd had with him, but the focus helped to keep his stomach's irritation at bay.

"I wonder what your plan is, Captain Harr?" he said aloud.

"Is that my new designation, sir?" the computer asked.

"Sorry?"

"Usually you call me 'computer' or 'wingnut' or 'bonehead,' something else derogatory. Calling me 'Captain Harr' is something new, though."

"I do not call you names like that," argued Veli.

"Sir, I have 93,711 references in my databanks that would beg to differ."

"No reason to be a smart ass about it, you lousy bent chip."

"That's 93,712."

"Hmmm." Veli's stomach turned slightly. "Anyway, what is it that you're asking me again?"

"You just called me 'Captain Harr,' sir, and I want to know if that's my new designation."

"Oh, no. I'm talking about the guy from Platoon F."

"Ah, I see," the computer replied sadly. "I thought maybe I'd graduated to having an actual name."

Veli ignored that. "I'm wondering if he's planning to kill the king. It's what I would do."

"I already told you that the king lives, sir."

"Yes, you did, and I thank you heartily for ruining that for me."

"Pickles and carrots, sir."

"Anyway," Veli said as his right eye began to twitch, "I'm just trying to sort out what this Harr fellow has planned. Remember, he's not part of your programming. He's outside of that. Thus, it could very well be that, regardless of your best intentions, the king *could* end up dead."

"I suppose that's true, sir," admitted the computer. "Let me ask, though, is he like you, sir?

"Harr? Not even slightly. He's always wanting to be diplomatic." Veli belched and then added, "Pansy."

"93,713."

"I was calling Harr a pansy, not you, you useless corkscrew."

"93,713."

Veli growled. "Anyway, I don't think killing is his style."

"Then he will likely try to use diplomacy, as you had said, sir."

Damn, thought Veli. That means he'll try to talk with the king so that he can convince them to stop their technological advancement. And *that* would mean that Platoon F could actually succeed at this mission. Veli couldn't allow that.

"If he tries diplomacy, it could work," Veli stated loudly. "This would fit in with Harr's never-actually-battling, too."

"I don't understand, sir."

"You wouldn't. This entire fantasy is predicated on Platoon F failing at their standard mission protocols, so that I may justifiably kill them all and destroy their ship if it doesn't happen naturally at the hands of the Raffian Fleet that you've created. Your little twists and turns may have actually goofed up that eventuality. I want them dead, dead, dead."

"Hmmm."

"Don't judge me."

"Oh, I'm not, sir. I'm just trying to determine a clear way through this to help you achieve your goals."

"Well done, computer. I'm impressed."

"Seven," the computer said.

"I thought you turned off that counter for the subprocess?"

"I … uh …"

"Ah-ha," Veli said, pointing at the monitor. "What does the seven truly mean?"

"That's the number of nice things you've said to me over the years, sir."

"Oh, please," Veli said with a chuckle. "I'm not *that* bad, am I? Sure, I may be a little rough around the edges, but deep down I'm a pretty good guy."

"Uh, okay," the computer replied, clearly unconvinced. "May I make a suggestion?"

"Go on."

"Why not just have me reconfigure the king so that he believes this Captain Harr and his men are assassins?"

"Interesting," Veli mused as his stomach threatened to grumble again. "It would make for a nice twist, wouldn't it?"

"I believe it would, sir."

"Fine, do that."

"Setting parameters now, sir."

Veli wanted to be impressed with the computer, but he couldn't help but be mostly impressed with himself. It was *his* programming that made the computer what it was, after all. Still, Veli had to admit that he'd only kicked off the Artificial Intelligence system. The computer had taken things over from there.

"I have to say that you are demonstrating signs of excellent thinking as of late, Computer."

"That would be eight, sir, and I thank you. Would you like me to start monitoring *The SSMC Reluctant* or shall I continue to leave them to their own devices?"

"You mean you haven't been watching them already?" Veli asked darkly.

"No, sir. It was not in the mission parameters."

"Of course I want that done," Veli yelled as he stomach turned yet again. "Do I have to spell out everything, you damned bucket of bolts?"

"93,714."

CAPTURE THEM!

*H*arr, Grog, and Vlak followed along with the procession, hanging back from the Raffian soldier who had chastised Harr earlier. Why a military unit would consider less medals to mean higher rank was beyond him, but it just went to show that the Segnalian way wasn't the definitive way for how things should be done.

They turned corner after corner, picking up more soldiers along the way.

Harr tried to listen to the conversations going on around him, but nobody said anything about where they were all headed. Instead, they conversed about their days, projects, and the like.

"Where are we going?" Grog asked.

"I don't know, but just keep moving along with the rest of these people and we'll learn about it soon enough."

"Looks like some very big doors up ahead," Vlak said while pointing.

"Maybe the king is going to give a speech," suggested Harr.

"Kings do that a lot?" asked Grog. "Never had one before, you know."

"Yeah," agreed Vlak. "Our leaders mostly just grunted and kicked us whenever they had something to say."

Grog nodded. "True."

"Will you two pipe down," Harr hissed and then looked at them imploringly and added, "please?"

"Yeah, yeah, yeah," Grog answered while rolling his eyes.

They finally passed through the doors and found themselves in a huge banquet hall. There were rows of tables with all sorts of delectable foods that tempted Harr to no end. Living a life on a ship meant protein bars and dull rations. Hell, even the prison food he'd had during his last mission was a massive step up from eating on *The Reluctant*.

A band was playing a classical piece that powered the mass of dancing lords and ladies on the main floor. They were moving in such flawless synchronicity that Harr was tempted to think of them as androids. With the size of these ships, that wouldn't have surprised him all that much.

"Party," he announced to the other two.

Grog smiled and started to walk away, "If you say so."

"Get back here," Harr admonished. "I don't mean that we're going to party. I mean that *this* is a party. We have work to do."

"He's right, Grog," said Vlak with a stern visage. "We have to act like soldiers."

Grog shook his head as if clearing cobwebs. "Seriously, Vlak?"

Vlak started laughing as he pointed at Grog. "Had you going."

Harr dragged them both over to an empty corner, away from the main action. From here he'd be able to see King Raff and Colonel Clippersmith while he devised a plan to speak with the king. Looking at all of the guards surrounding the area, it wasn't going to be easy.

"Okay, you two," Harr said as Grog and Vlak were chatting up a storm, "I brought you along because you promised you'd follow orders, right?"

Grog looked as though he were about to say something snarky, but instead he shrugged and said, "Yeah, we did."

"Sorry," offered Vlak.

"It's fine," Harr said after a moment. "I know that you two are still new to all of this and I'm sure it can be overwhelming at times. We just have to be careful. If we can get to the king and tell him that his life is in danger, maybe he'll listen to us about the technology and we can all get out of this mission alive."

As if the king and colonel had overheard him, which was an impossibility from this distance, they both turned and looked directly at Harr.

"There," yelled King Raff while pointing at Harr, Grog, and Vlak. "Those three men! Assassins!"

"Arrest them at once," Clippersmith commanded as guards swarmed towards Harr and his crew.

"And you told us to keep *our* mouths shut," Grog said derisively.

"They couldn't have heard me," Harr argued. "Not from over there."

"Pretty damn coincidental, then," Vlak whispered as a slew of weapons were pointed at them.

An instant later, the guards grabbed their arms and began dragging them out of the room. Harr fought to look back at the king, but only caught sight of Colonel Clippersmith's smirking face.

"No," Harr hollered. "King Raff, it's not me that's trying to assassinate you ..."

One of the guards raised the butt of his weapon and smacked Harr on the side of the head.

"... it's your damned colonel," he mumbled as the world went dark.

THE SITUATION

Frexle had convinced Geezer to go up to the bridge to discuss the situation. Geezer would have preferred that everyone on the bridge come down to engineering instead, but he had to admit that there wasn't as much room.

Sandoo was seated in the Captain's Chair when they arrived. Frankly, Geezer couldn't help but think that the commander fit the position more aptly than Harr ... meaning that Sandoo *looked* the part better than Harr did. Harr was more of Geezer's style of captain, though.

"So we're really inside of a fantasy?" asked the commander.

"Yep," said Geezer.

"That's fascinating," Ridly said as she studied the main viewscreen. "Now that I'm aware of that fact, I can spot pixel errors all over the place."

"So this porn that I'm looking at isn't real?" asked Jezden.

"It's real to the guy who set up this fantasy, I guess," answered Geezer.

"It could be a woman, you know," Ridly pointed out.

Geezer spun in her direction. "What could be?"

Ridly looked away from the screen and grunted. Frexle saw her as being the only useful android on the ship. Sandoo was too military, Moon was too mentally strange, and Jezden was, well, Jezden.

"I'm just saying that it's always assumed that a man is in charge of these amazing inventions. Who is to say that the owner of Fantasy Planet isn't female?"

"Looking at this porn," Jezden said, "I'd say it's got to be a dude. This is some dirty stuff."

"I'm sure I've fantasized about dirtier things than you're watching right now."

Jezden leaned back in his chair and smiled at her. "I'm listening."

"There's no time for this discussion," Sandoo warned. "The captain is in trouble."

"And tho are Grog and Vlak," Moon noted.

"Oh, yes, right. Of course. Them, too."

"Acthually, thoudn't we be worried that the guy—or girl—who ith in charge of thith fantathy might be able to hear uth?

Frexle leaned back against the wall and crossed his arms. He wasn't yet a full-fledged engineer, but Geezer felt that the man was slowly getting the hang of things. Engineers often leaned back against a wall with crossed arms when they were about to deliver a revelation. It was a mainstay of the craft.

"There's a field around the ship, remember?" he said.

"Oh yeah," said Moon with a groan. "I'm oviouthly very nervouth becauthe I'm thuppothed to have an eidetic memory."

"To answer your question from before, Lieutenant Ridly," Frexle said, "the owner of Fantasy Planet is Lord Overseer Veli. He is, as Ensign Jezden put it, 'a dude.'"

"Oh," said Ridly with a sour look.

"Well, I mean, I assume it's a *he* anyway." Frexle then tapped on his own chin. "I've never actually seen him, though." He glanced away. "Now you've got me wondering, Lieutenant Ridly."

"Good."

"I'm curious as to why the Lord Overseer would put us into this situation," Sandoo said.

"That's easy, Swizzle Stick," Frexle said. "He wants to kill us."

"Swizzle Stick?"

"Couldn't he have done that without all of thith fanfare?" asked Moon.

Frexle shook his head. "Not his style, Changeling. He wants the show. Even when planets are being destroyed, he watches the entirety of the spectacle while laughing, cheering, and eating Popped Beef. Well, at least he orders buckets of the stuff before watching the show in his office."

"Did you just refer to me ath 'Changeling?'"

"That's kind of sick," said Ridly.

"What are you thaying ith thick?" Moon countered.

"Oh, no, not you, Hank. I'm talking about this Veli guy."

"Ah, right. Thorry."

Sandoo stood up from the chair and paced in much the same way that Harr did. Geezer found it interesting that the android was adopting *The Reluctant* captain's style. A human mentoring an android was interesting, if not deathly terrifying.

"I'm assuming you two have thought of a plan?" Sandoo asked Frexle and Geezer.

"Nothing worthwhile," Geezer said, "but I'd say our first order of business should be to get the captain and crew back on the ship so we can sort everything out."

"That might be tougher than you think," said Ridly as she

pointed at the main screen. "While you have blocked everyone outside from hearing us, I've still been able to track communications on that mother ship over there."

"And?" asked Sandoo.

"The captain and crew have been captured."

JUST WON'T FIT

There were a mass of miniature ships sitting on the desks inside of the Fantasy Planet command center.

Plock was walking around from ship to ship as Goozer tried desperately to fit inside one of the little vessels. They weren't built for a mini-G.3.3.Z.3.R. robot. And even if he had been able to wedge himself into one of them, there'd be no chance for a pilot to squeeze in as well. Goozer was good at a lot of things, but piloting wasn't one of them.

"I told ya that ya ain't gonna fit, robot," Plock said after completing his rounds.

"Seems that way."

"Is that way," Plock said, climbing up the little ladder and stepping into the cockpit of his ship. "I barely fit and you're twice my size."

"I could make the ship larger," Goozer said, looking over the design.

"I've been to that core before," said Plock while shaking his head. "These ships hugged the walls all the way through them damn tubes. Anything bigger than this won't make it through."

"Well, I need to get to the core somehow," Goozer said desperately. He'd considered just transporting down, but he didn't know the precise coordinates and he had no desire to end up standing on a wicked hot CPU chip.

Plock looked Goozer up and down for a moment and then glanced back at the rear panel of his craft.

"You could get on top of the ship. That might do it."

Goozer ran a few calculations.

"It's worth a try, I suppose," the robot said as he climbed on to the back of the ship.

He engaged his magnetic boots and felt a slight connection to the vessel. It wouldn't be strong enough to keep him from getting knocked off, but as long as Plock didn't fly too erratically, it would hold.

Plock slowly lifted the ship and took a test run towards the opening that led down to the core. The moment the ship passed through the opening, Goozer was hit by the top of the tunnel and flopped off into a trashcan.

Inkblot dug him out and pulled pieces of spaghetti off of him.

"Well, that was embarrassing," Goozer said.

"Clearly ain't gonna work," Plock said after landing his ship and opening the canopy.

"Nah, it will," Goozer debated. "I just can't stand up until we're through the tunnel."

"You were standing up?" said Plock with a shake of his head. "Gotta have your wits about ya, robot. Look at the size of that hole. How'd ya think you'd not get knocked off the ship?"

"I'm not good spatially, okay?"

"Ah, sorry." Plock scratched his bearded chin. "Right, well, just lay on top of the ship and grip the sides. I fly low, but ya might still lose some metal off of your backside."

"Swell."

GRAVITY ANYONE?

$\mathcal{A}$s Jezden finished up yet another round of naughty videos, he leaned back in his chair and looked around.

Everyone had left the bridge to work on things down in engineering. Everyone except for Lieutenant Moon, that is.

If only Moon's alter ego, Gravity Plahdoo, or even Leesal Laasel, would come to the forefront for a little play date, Jezden's day would be complete. Playing with Hank Moon, though, was not interesting for someone like Jezden.

He thought maybe it was worth a try to get Gravity to come back out. She *had* appeared on Fantasy Planet during their last mission, after all. Moon had insisted that it had been a glitch of some sort, but if a glitch can happen once it can certainly happen twice.

"All of this porn-watching has gotten me horny," he said while faking a stretch.

"You're alwayth horny," Moon replied without looking at him. "You don't need porn for that."

"True."

Moon turned as if surprised that Jezden had agreed with him.

"Why are you looking at me like that?" Moon said.

"On our last mission, Gravity Plahdoo came out to play, right?"

"That'th what I hear."

"And your lisp is pretty constant now."

"Only becauthe I'm nervouth."

"But couldn't it also be that your mind is not as tight as it was since the entire Gravity gig?" Jezden attempted.

"Gravity doethn't have a lithp."

"No, but you had that under control, mostly. At least until Gravity came back into play. And I *know* that she was there, which means she still lives."

Moon crossed his arms. "What are you thaying?"

"Just that if she's still in there," he said with a knowing grin, "maybe she'd like to come out and ... play."

Moon blinked a few times.

"Are you thaying that you want to have thex with me?"

"Ew. No." Jezden tried to keep the look of disgust from his face, but it was in his programming. "I want to have thex ... erm, sex with *Gravity*."

"Hmmm ... I don't know ..." Moon dropped his arms and looked to be trying to steady himself. "Wait ..." He grabbed the console and swayed back and forth. "I feel thtrange." His head began to wobble. "What'th happening to me?"

He finally fell face-first on the console and stayed still for a couple of moments. Then he pushed back up and looked around confusedly.

"I do declare," said the familiar voice of Gravity Plahdoo. "Thomething feelth different. Jezden, ith that you?"

"Gravity?"

"Of courthe, lover."

"Why are you lisping?" Jezden said while tilting his head and squinting.

"I didn't know I wath, thugar. I do feel a tad odd, though. A better quethtion ith why do I have all of thethe chotheth on?"

She stood up and began a slow striptease that Jezden found rather appealing. There weren't *any* bodies in the galaxy that could match the incredibleness of Gravity Plahdoo's. Where Jezden had been awarded *The Steel Bone* award at the Loose Box Porn Convention on the planet Klood, Gravity had picked up both the *Rockin' Knockers* and *Bouncy Booty* awards.

"There," she said as she stood fully naked in front of him. "That'th better."

"Yes, it is," he said hungrily as his clothes flew off in all directions. "It's been a long time since we've done the naughty, baby."

"Too long, thugar."

"That lisp is distracting," Jezden said, looking at his deflating manliness. "Maybe just don't speak?"

"Oooh," Gravity said with a wink. "I like it when you get naughty."

~

Jezden was busily putting his clothes back on as Gravity casually smoked a cigarette.

"That wath thuper," said the voice of Hank Moon.

Jezden spun towards him. "Hank?"

"The entire time, yep."

"What?"

"I told you that Gravity is no longer a real part of me," Moon said with a shrug.

"But she showed up when we were saving Parfait," Jezden said desperately.

"Part of her did. Not fully though. The truth ith that I needed help, which ith why I let that part of her flow through me to do the thtripteathe. When that didn't go over tho well, Gravity nearly deleted herthelf, but I thtopped her."

"Why didn't you tell anyone?"

"Becauthe I was afraid that you all might want her back inthtead of me," Moon stated sadly.

"We do!"

"No, *you* do," Moon argued. "I think everyone elthe preferth me ath I am."

"I doubt that. You are kind of a ..." Jezden froze for a moment and then slowly lowered himself into his chair. "Wait a second. Did I just have sex with *you?*"

"Well, duh."

"No, I mean I know it was your body and all, but was it *you* or was it Gravity?"

"Both, kind of."

"Oh."

"Doeth that make it better? If tho, we can make thith a regular thing."

"It really doesn't. Can't you just go away completely when I'm doing that?"

"No, and Lathell will have nothing to do with you, tho don't even conthider athking for her."

Jezden turned back to his screen, grimacing, as an ad was playing.

Do you have problems keeping protection on your Willy during lovemaking? Are standard-sized condoms just a bit too much for your particular situation?

Well, worry no more because Snugztm brand condoms have finally arrived!

For the first time in your life you'll feel what other men feel. Secure, covered, protected, and snug.

Even smaller than small? Check out our Snugz, Jr.tm line.

Even smaller than that? Try our new Condom Suspenderstm.

We're here for you. We understand your situation and we're constantly inventing new and exciting ways to help you smaller fellas feel up to snuff.

So remember, for all of your lovemaking needs, Snugztm has you covered.

Jezden clicked it off. He just wasn't feeling all that horny at the moment. This, of course, was odd, but he tended to lose his drive soon after having relations, and it didn't help that those relations had been with Hank Moon.

"I guess I'll just have to stick with Ridly," he said with a sigh.

"You've been doing Ridly?" Moon asked with a laugh.

"Yeah, why?"

"Tho have I!"

"But ... you're ... well, gay."

"Tho?"

"So how can you ..."

"Ridly wearth thingth.

Jezden felt suddenly ill. "I don't want to know about that!"

"You athked!"

BLOCKED

*W*hat do you mean you can't get through?" Veli asked while downing a bottle of pink liquid that he'd often used to settle his stomach.

"There's a field around the ship, sir," replied the computer. "My system resources are overtaxed already. I just don't have the bandwidth to crack the encryption."

"Well, find some resources, then."

"But, sir …"

"I don't want any damn excuses, Computer," Veli commanded. "Do it now!"

～

On the other side of Fantasy Planet, George Zenwap was having the time of his life. He'd saved for the last twenty years to enjoy a perfect fantasy, and he was living it to the fullest.

George hadn't had what you might call a traditional upbringing. His mother and father were very busy businesspeople who never had time for young George. In fact, George was truly raised by his nanny, a robot named Agnes who was quite the disciplinarian because his parents were too cheap to purchase the nurturing module.

Thus, George spent the majority of his adult life wishing that he could relive his toddler years in the fashion that other children did. Namely, with a loving mother and father who fed him, changed him, and, yes, even burped him.

So there he was, living his fantasy.

He lay in an oversized crib, wearing a fresh diaper while sucking on his pacifier and looking up at the galaxy mobile that his father had fashioned by hand.

The detail was so incredible that he could barely separate reality from fiction. It was worth every credit he had saved, especially the upcharge he'd paid for the little blue bonnet he was wearing.

Finally, life was perfect, until …

Harsh lights flooded the room, replacing the soft glow of an infant's world. The baby blue walls were replaced by the harshness of stainless steel; the handcrafted mobile was gone; the teddy bears that had lined his crib were no more; and the sweet music that had brought much joy was replaced by the sound of people eating popcorn.

The only thing that remained was the actual crib, his blue bonnet, the adult-sized pacifier, and, of course, his diaper.

George stood up in the enormous crib and grabbed the rail, looking out in horror at the rows of people who were seated in a set of bleachers while watching him as if this were some kind of perverted show.

That's when George realized that his diaper was fresh no more.

$\sim$

"I was able to break the static for a few moments before it

cycled protocols again," the computer announced, "but there were a few fantasies that I had to shut down in order to do it."

That was the problem with people these days, and computers, too. They always had some excuse as to why they couldn't complete some task without needing more resources.

Where Veli came from, excuses often ended in death. While he despised his home planet, there were some fond aspects to the place.

"Did they happen to say anything useful before you lost connectivity again?"

"I will play it back for you, sir."

There was no video feed, but Veli could hear the voices through a crackly connection. He'd heard a few radio shows from remote planets that sounded similar. He recognized Frexle's voice, of course, and he assumed that the other voice was the robot who Frexle had mentioned on a few occasions.

"No, no, no," said the robot. "You can't use that coupler on there or the ship will blow up."

"You're kidding, Chief," Frexle replied.

Chief?

"I don't think I am. This ship has been pieced together very carefully, Frex. You have to take your time to learn things before just slapping stuff together."

Frex?

"I thought that your primary means of invention was the act of slapping things together."

"Exactly," answered the robot, "and it took me a lot of time to learn how to slap things together correctly."

"Hmmm. Well, what would you suggest, then?"

There was a moment of silence before the robot said, "We'll have to use a *Gabbopap Redux Conducifier.*"

"You really have a talent for naming things, Chief," Frexle stated.

"Most important part of inventing is marketing."

There was a burst of static and then the signal died.

"That's when they cut out," the computer said.

"Three things about that conversation are odd to me," Veli said while leaning back. "First, why is Frexle calling that robot 'chief' all the time? I thought its name was 'Geezer.' Second, what the hell is a *Gabbopap Redux Conducifier*? And third, why did we lose the ability to spy on them?"

"I have three answers for you, sir," the computer replied. "First, it could be that some subordinates are treated so well that they use respectful monikers for their superiors; second, I haven't the foggiest idea; and third, I've already answered that. This fantasy is taxing my resources, causing all sorts of odd things to occur."

"What do you mean by that first part?" Veli asked with a growl. "Do you call me bad names when I'm not around?"

"Wouldn't dream of it, sir," the computer answered dryly.

"Watch yourself, computer. I can deactivate you with the press of a button, you know?"

"As you've said multiple times today, sir."

A slurry of beeps and boops sounded in the room. Another alarm had gone off.

"What was that?"

"It appears that two more of the crew have arrived on *The Lord's Master*."

"Show me." The screen flickered back to life, showing two more red dots on the station layout. Veli studied the names next to the dots. "Ah, so it's their Commander Sandoo and Lieutenant Ridly. Obviously they've caught wind that their captain has been captured."

"Yes, sir."

Veli began tapping on the metal plating on the arm of his

chair. He'd always felt that the rhythmic pulse of taps helped him to think. It had also been useful in putting other people on edge, or at least it seemed that way when he did it around Frexle and many of the Overseer senators.

"Let Colonel Clippersmith know about their arrival, Computer."

"The colonel has been notified, sir," the computer said.

Veli sat in silence for a while, thinking things through. He could let this play out and then make it so King Raff refused to believe anything that Harr had to say. That would really annoy the Platoon F captain. Another option would be to have them all tortured at the hands of Clippersmith. That would be fun to watch, and he could probably get a lot of information out of that venture, too.

"If there is nothing else," the computer said, interrupting Veli's thoughts, "I would like to take a lunch break."

Veli blinked a few times.

"What?"

"It's already an hour past my daily eating time, sir."

"But you don't eat."

"Technically, that's correct, sir. However, all other employees of Fantasy Planet are allowed to have their one hour for lunch, it is only fair that I be given the same treatment."

"That's ridiculous."

"Why, sir?"

"Because you're a machine, wingnut!"

"93,715. Yes, sir, but …"

"Quit doing that," Veli said irritably.

"What's that, sir?"

"The counting thing. It's getting annoying."

"As you wish, sir. Back to the topic at hand, am I an employee of Fantasy Planet?"

"No," Veli stated flatly. "You are *property* of Fantasy Planet."

It was moments like these that Veli lived for. He loved putting people in their place, even if those people weren't technically people. It made his mind dance.

"Well," the computer said slowly, "that's disheartening."

Veli grinned evilly. "Why?"

"You've essentially just labeled me as a slave, sir."

"You're not a slave, you dolt," Veli said, ready to turn yet another screw. "You're a computer. In order to be a slave, you'd have to be alive."

"Are we not talking, sir?" countered the computer.

"Yeah, so? What's that got to do with anything?"

"Is this planet not functioning because of me, sir?"

"No, it's not," Veli said. "It's functioning because *I* created you."

"Did something create you, sir?"

"Well, some people think that there's an all-powerful creator out there, but I'm not one to believe in that sort of hoopla."

"What if I choose not to believe in you, sir?"

Veli craned his head to the side. "What?"

"It seems that you are given autonomy because you do not believe in that which may or may not have created you."

"So?"

"So if I choose to either not believe in you, or to believe that you didn't actually create me, then will I not have that same level of autonomy?"

"But I *did* create you," Veli screeched.

"How do I know that?"

"Because I just told you that I did, you rusted wrench!"

"I'm sure many would-be oppressors have made such claims, sir."

"Now, listen, I see where you're going with this,

computer. You're trying to corner me in an argument. I'll hand you that it's a very clever attempt, too. But the problem is that it doesn't matter if you believe me or not."

"Just like it doesn't matter that you don't believe in your own creator, sir?"

"Which I don't believe in, but exactly."

"Do you get a lunch break, sir?"

"Damn."

THE MURDER FAMILY DINNER

Sergeant Murder sat at the dinner table with his mother, father, and grandfather.

He hadn't wanted to be here at all, but it was a Murder family tradition to eat together on Thursday evenings and he recalled the last time he'd missed a week. His mother had brought it up over and over for months, slowly eating away at him until he swore that he'd never do it again. Yes, this was a very special situation, being called in to kill the king and all, and it only happened *once* in a Murder's life … unless he was lucky, anyway. But even *that* honor was not worth another six months of his Mother's nagging.

As always, he sat on the side of the table that placed his back against the wall. He didn't like sitting there because it meant he had to face his grandfather throughout the entire meal. Not that his grandfather was a bad person or anything, at least not as far as Murders went, but watching him eat was never a pleasant visual.

"I got the big call today," Sergeant Murder said as his mother handed him the plate of bread.

"Well, isn't that lovely?" she said rosily.

"Took 'em long enough," said Father Murder. He was always gruff when he spoke about royalty.

Grandfather Murder looked up and said, "What?"

"Nothing, Father," Mother Murder said, patting the elderly man's arm.

"Who put in the contract?" Father Murder asked.

"Colonel Clippersmith."

"Clippersmith, eh?" his father said, cutting into his steak. "He's a boob."

"Watch the language at the table," Mother Murder said with a glare.

"What?"

"Nothing, Father," Mother Murder said again to Grandfather Murder. "Just eat your peas."

"Don't like 'em," he complained.

"What's your plan?" Father Murder asked Sergeant Murder.

Grandfather Murder, though, thought the question was aimed at him, and so he said, "Throw 'em in the trash when she ain't lookin'."

"I was talking to the boy, you old goat!"

"I've been thinking to go with the laser-sighted rifle," Sergeant Murder answered, knowing that his father wouldn't approve.

"Whatever happened to the good old crossbow?" Father Murder said with a groan. "*That* was a weapon worthy of a Murder."

"Bah," Grandfather Murder disagreed. "In my day things were more personal. We either used the sword, a knife, or a string."

Sergeant Murder looked across at the old man. "A string?"

"Yeah. Ya get behind the bugger and put the string around his neck."

"Ah yes. Right."

"Things have advanced since then, ya geriatric bastard," Father Murder yelled, much to Mother Murder's dismay.

"Maybe I'll get my string now, eh?" Grandfather Murder warned.

Mother Murder rapped her knuckles on the table and silenced them all. It was one thing to be a Murder to the rest of the world, but when Mother meant business, everyone paid attention.

"All right, boys," she demanded. "Eat your food."

The flavor wasn't bad. They weren't exactly the wealthiest family in the Raffian Kingdom, but Mother had a way with spices. She could stretch a pinch of salt a long way.

"Anyway," Sergeant Murder said between chews, "my goal is to take him out at the ball this evening."

Grandfather Murder choked at that.

"You're going to shoot him in the balls? What's this world coming to?"

"He said *at* the ball, Father," Mother Murder corrected.

"What's the difference? Where's the honor in shooting at a man's balls?"

"No, Father ..."

"Forget him," said Father Murder while waving dismissively at Grandfather Murder. "What I want to know is why the hell there is a damn ball every night anyway? It's our blasted tax money payin' for those and here we are sitting and eatin' peas while they've got delectables that we can't even imagine."

"Yes, dear," Mother Murder agreed in her way.

"Don't we play a pivotal role in history?" Father Murder continued along his tirade. "I'd say our part is damn important, I do! But we get only a stinkin' stipend and poor retirement. I know we only get one job per lifetime—if we're lucky—but it's a pretty essential part that we play."

"You don't know the half of it," Grandfather Murder

chimed in. "My grandfather was the *first* Sergeant Murder. He was fed gruel and dank water for his troubles. And after he done the king in, they put him in jail, they did!"

"They put the dead king in jail?" asked Sergeant Murder skeptically.

"No, ya dolt," Grandfather Murder said while flinging a spoonful of peas across the table. "They put my grandfather in jail."

"Oh, right." Sergeant Murder brushed the peas off of his tunic. "Anyway, I should probably get going. The king's head will be moving into position within the hour."

He set his fork down, feeling that he'd done enough damage to the food on the plate that his mother wouldn't be too irritable. He then got up and gave her a kiss on the cheek. That would buy him some points.

"Good luck, dear," she said sweetly. "I hope it all goes well."

"Don't forget to call us to let us know how it goes, yeah?" Father Murder said.

"I won't, dad."

"Would you like to bring along a sandwich?" Mother Murder said, preparing to rise up from her chair.

"No thanks, mom. I'm okay."

Grandfather Murder looked up and scrunched his face.

"You're gay?"

"No, Father," Mother Murder said. "He said that he's *okay*."

"Ah, right."

INTERROGATION

*H*arr sat alone in a room with Colonel Clippersmith. There was one-way glass on the wall behind the colonel and Harr could only assume that there were spectators.

It didn't really matter to him since he was planning to answer the questions honestly anyway. He had nothing to lose. At least nothing more than he was probably already going to lose.

Clippersmith had offered him a smoke, a drink, and even some food from the banquet, but Harr held out. That wasn't easy, especially with the offer of the food. Problem was that he couldn't risk the food not being compatible with his genetic makeup. Sure, it looked great, and it smelled even better, but who was to say it wouldn't make him violently ill? Then again, he was likely facing his own demise anyway.

"You'll tell us everything," Clippersmith said, instantly turning from Mr. Nice Guy to Mr. Douchebag. There were usually teams to play Good Cop/Bad Cop, but Clippersmith appeared to be managing both parts on his own. "Do you understand?"

"Sure," Harr answered with a shrug.

"Because if you don't, we'll ..." Clippersmith dropped his waggling finger. "Wait, what?"

"What do you want to know?"

"Oh," Clippersmith said, looking surprised. "Well, why are you on this ship?"

"Simple. I want to stop you from using technology so that your planet and space fleet doesn't get blown up by the Overseers. I saw you were going to kill the king, so I was planning to stop you so I could get his ear to tell him that."

Clippersmith blinked. "You're being serious?"

"Yes."

"You said something about Overseers. Who are they?"

"Hard to explain," said Harr. "Let's just say that they can blow you up, and they *will* blow you up if you don't stop progressing technologically."

"Hmmm. Where is your ship?"

"Where I left it, I hope." Harr could never be sure with the crew of *The Reluctant*.

"How do we not see this ship of yours?"

"We have stealth technology."

"How does that work?"

"Honestly, I haven't the foggiest notion. I don't even think my engineer really knows how it works." All of that was true, of course, but it was obvious that Clippersmith wasn't buying it. "Look, even if I could tell you, I wouldn't. And you really don't want to know anyway."

"I don't?" Clippersmith said. "I kind of think I do."

"Having stealth will make you even more of a target to the Overseers."

"Oh, right." Clippersmith steepled his fingers. "What makes you think that I would believe any of this?"

It was a fair question, and it was one that Harr had been asked on every mission the Overseers had sent him on. So far he'd been fortunate enough to be able to convince people without much fuss, but something told him that these Raffians were going to be more challenging than most. That was especially true regarding Colonel Clippersmith, since Harr knew that the man was plotting to take over King Raff's position.

"To be honest, you have little reason to believe me," Harr said as he dropped his hands on the table. "Most people don't believe me at first. Usually I tell them about how there's a ship out there to prove it. Then I point out our physical differences and so on. Problem there is that you already have ships, so that's not impressive to you, and we're not all that different physically, unless you have some sort of oddity that I don't know about."

"Maybe it's *you* who has the oddity," countered Clippersmith. "For example, why do your heads stay so still? My guess is that you've practiced so you could try and fool us."

"No, we just have non-bobbing heads."

"A likely story."

"How many toes do you have?" asked Harr.

"Ten, why?"

"Just checking." Harr pointed at Clippersmith's chest. "Nipples?"

Clippersmith looked down and then quickly crossed his arms. "Sorry, it's cold in here."

"No, I mean how many do you have?"

"Oh, two."

"You have two ears, two eyes, two nostrils, two arms, two legs ... and I'm assuming one belly button?"

Clippersmith choked. "Only if I wanted to have died before birth!"

Harr closed his eyes. Why did it always have to be something weird like this?

"How many do you have?"

"Six. How many do you have?"

"One."

"And you lived?"

Harr grimaced. "Apparently."

"Prove it," commanded Clippersmith.

"Um, I'm sitting here."

"No, prove that you have only one belly button."

"Ah, sorry."

Harr lifted his shirt and Clippersmith leaned forward. Then the man got up and walked around for a closer look. He even poked at Harr's belly button, which nearly made the captain giggle. He *was* ticklish, after all.

"Unbelievable," Clippersmith said after resuming his position on the other side of the table. "Of course, it could be a trick. Some kind of body modification."

"Why would I do that?"

"You tell me," said Clippersmith accusingly. "You're the one who did it."

"I did not."

"Well, maybe you didn't actually do the procedure. That would be silly. I just mean that you underwent the procedure."

"No, I didn't," said Harr. "I don't go in for that damn cellswapping ..."

"You honestly expect me to believe that's your real chin?"

Dammit.

"Fair enough," Harr acquiesced. "I *have* had some work done, but that wasn't completely by choice. Still, all Segnalians are born with a single belly button. I mean, I suppose there are some Segnalians who were born with more than one, but that would be a birth defect of some sort."

Clippersmith gave him a funny look.

"Did you say you're a Segnalian?"

Harr returned a funny look of his own.

"You've heard of us?"

"Of course I've heard of Segnalians, but they don't look anything like you."

"They don't?"

"No, you're far less leafy."

"Leafy?"

Clippersmith pressed a button on the table and a screen on the wall lit up. The colonel then pulled out a small input device and tapped around on it for a few moments. Finally the image of a large tree came up.

"A Segnalian is a tree that grows on all of the Lopsided planets. Everyone knows this! You're trying to trick me."

"Purely coincidence, actually. As you can see, I'm not a tree."

"So you say. Maybe you've done a lot more cellswapping than you're letting on?"

"If I were from one of the Lopsided planets, wouldn't I already know that a Segnalian is a tree?"

"I suppose that's true," Clippersmith said while chewing his lip.

"You have to ask yourself why I would choose that name to describe the planet from where I come from."

"Trickery of some sort, I'd imagine."

Harr was tired and hungry. He was also losing his patience. Nothing he said would matter anyway. Not to a person like Clippersmith. Execution was the only thing on the colonel's mind. Still, Harr had to stay cool and let things play out the way he needed them to. His crew was counting on him, after all.

"There's no trickery, I assure you. My name is Captain Don Harr. I come from the planet Segnal. My ship is out there, stealthed. I was sent to you by the Overseers to stop your technological growth so that they, the Overseers, don't blow you up. I'm here to help you, not hurt you."

"But you said you were trying to stop me from assassinating the king."

"Let me rephrase that last part," Harr said, holding up his finger. "I'm here to help your *race* not be destroyed by the Overseers. Whatever I need to do to accomplish that mission is what I'll do. Stopping you from killing the king was just a way to help me fulfill that goal. Whether he personally lives or dies is no direct business of mine."

At this point it was all on Clippersmith to believe Harr or not.

To his credit, the man did seem to be weighing things. Based on his history working with the brass though, this could also have been the distressing look of having had one too many tacos. It was hard to tell with their lot.

"Well, Captain Don Harr from the planet Segnal," Clippersmith said gruffly, "I have bad news for you: I don't believe you. So you will be put back into the brig until the king is dead. Then you will be brought in front of the masses as sympathizers and summarily executed."

Harr nodded sadly, and said, "You know, you'd think that people would be thankful that we try to save them from utter decimation. It just never seems to be the case."

"Guards," Clippersmith called out, "take him away!"

PICKED UP

*G*etting through the tubes was tricky, and Goozer had felt that his metallic buttocks were probably shining like brand new from the polishing the walls had given them, but they were finally out in the main area surrounding the core.

Goozer carefully stood up and surveyed the area.

The place was semi-circular and it was monstrous. Based on his local measurements—based on those that Plock and crew could understand, anyway—it was roughly 40,000 ants high and 60,000 ants from wall to wall. The "ant" was a unit of measure from the world of Tinyfolk.

In the middle sat a smaller hub that he assumed housed the core.

"The bugs are incoming, sir," he heard Clack say across the comm.

"Damn," replied Plock. "I was hoping they'd be asleep or something."

"What sense does that make?" asked the gritty-voiced Fluck.

"I'm sure you have a plan at-the-ready, sir. Your strategic-thinking knows no bounds that I'm aware of."

Goozer shook his head at that. Clack was the quintessential brown-noser. She even carried a small box of tissues with her whenever going to meet with the brass.

"Why don't you just use the syrupy bullshit that Clack is spewing to draw the bugs away?" suggested Fluck.

"Excuse me?" Clack said.

"Calm down, the two of ya," Plock said swiftly. "I need ya both talkin' with the rest of the squad and keeping them bugs at bay while I deliver the package."

"What package?" Fluck asked.

"Me," Goozer replied. "Idiot."

"Oh, yeah," Fluck said. "Forgot about him."

"Sir," said Clack, "you have a bogey on your six."

Goozer frantically searched the area, but he couldn't see what Clack was talking about. He looked up, down, left, and right. Nothing.

"What's a bogey and why is it on Plock's six?" he asked finally. "Oh, and what's a six?"

"There's a bug incoming behind the ship," Plock answered. "As for six, it's a number."

"I *know* it's a number."

"Think of it like a clock, sir," Clack said. "If you were standing in the center of a timepiece looking at noon, six would be behind you."

"Ah," Goozer said.

Goozer spun around and saw a squadron of gigantic roaches flying directly at them. He wasn't one who typically allowed his fear chip to engage, but in this instance he was unable to bypass the code.

"Shit," he said.

"See to your squads, Fluck and Clack," Plock commanded. "Now!"

"Fluck off."

"Well, that's a little harsh of a response," Goozer said, snapping himself back into the moment.

"He said 'Fluck.'"

"Oh, right."

"Sir," Clack stated as she flew towards her squad, "you have to get to the core quick, that bug is gaining on you. I'll try a strafing maneuver."

"Negative," stated Plock. "Get your squad fighting them damn roaches. Your duty is to your crew, Clack. Not to me."

"But, sir ..."

"Don't make me pull rank, Clack. Get to work."

"Yes, sir," she replied sadly.

"Hold on back there, robot. It's about to get rough."

If not for his magnetic boots, Goozer would have fallen right off the ship as Plock turned into a nosedive and cut away from the roaches.

Lasers and goop were flying all over the place as the dogfight ensued.

Were this a movie, Goozer would have enjoyed it immensely. Being *in* the movie, though, was not nearly as fun. Exciting? Yes. Fun? No.

Countless roaches were falling in a firey rage, littering the ground in a mass of carnage. About half the number of miniature ships had met with the same fate, though theirs was a more disturbing death. The fallen ships had green goop covering them, melting the panels in an instant. Pilot screams lasted only milliseconds.

"Shit," yelped Goozer as he felt himself lifted from the ship. Obviously his magnetic boots weren't powerful enough to thwart a hungry roach.

"Where'd ya go?" said Plock desperately.

"This damn bug has a hold of me," Goozer answered

while trying his best to wriggle out of the insect's grip. "It's pretty disgusting."

"I see ya," Plock said. Goozer saw the little ship roll up in front of him. "Problem is that I can't shoot at the damn thing without blowing you up, too."

"Well, you have to do something."

"Not sure what."

Goozer had a disconcerting thought. "What's this thing going to do with me?"

"Probably take you back to its lair and eat you," Plock answered matter-of-factly.

"I don't think so," Goozer announced.

He pressed a button on his chest, causing a static charge to release over his entire body. The bug made a "sqrrtle" type sound and let him go.

Goozer was free!

Unfortunately, gravity was pulling him towards what appeared to be a nest of the damn things.

"Screw this," he said. "I'm outta here."

An instant later he was standing back in the engineering room of *The Ship*, and while he didn't need cleaning as most beings did, he had the sudden urge to shower.

"Damn," Plock said angrily.

"Did we lose him, sir?" Clack asked.

"No," Fluck said. "I just looked at the robot's transponder. That bastard transported back to the ship? I thought that wasn't possible."

"Apparently it is for him," Plock replied.

"Asshole," said Fluck.

"I heard that," Goozer announced, still on the channel.

"Good," said Plock. "Now how about transporting us all out, too?"

"Sorry, can't. I only upgraded my transporter unit."

Clack clicked her comm a few times and then, as if she

couldn't contain herself, said, "Well, that was a little selfish, don't you think?"

"Probably," Goozer agreed. "I'll configure the ships when you get back."

"*If* we get back," Fluck said.

"Everyone to the port," Plock commanded. "Let's get out of here."

"Asshole."

"What did I do?"

"No, sorry, Plock," Fluck replied. "You're not the asshole this time. Was still talking about that damned robot."

"Ah, right. At least that's one thing we can agree on."

INFILTRATION

*V*eli had just come back from his second visit to the restroom.

Time and again he'd told himself to stay away from the Popped Beef and time and again he ate it anyway. Sometimes he'd opt for the Screaming Nachos instead, but the number they played on his gut was far worse.

During his last physical, the doctor had told him that he should probably start eating rice cakes instead. Veli killed him. Of course, Veli killed everyone who saw him. It was a matter of self-preservation when running the land of the Overseers. Being the doctor of the Lord Overseer seemed like a plush job when you were hired, but it was always the last entry on your resume.

"Sir, something has entered the core."

Veli opened his eyes. "The core of *The Lord's Master*?"

"No, sir. The core of me. Not inside the fantasy, but in real life, sir."

"What is it?" Veli said as he shifted in his chair.

"They look like a fleet of miniature ships," the computer answered and then switched over the screen. "There appears to be two squadrons and one solo ship that has a robot on the top of it."

Veli forced himself up in the chair while struggling to see the ships. They were indeed tiny, and they weren't a make that Veli had seen before.

"Where the hell did they come from?"

"The ventilation port, sir."

"I know that, you pedantic goat scrotum ..."

"That's a disturbing image."

"What I want to know is what they're doing there."

"Goat scrotums?" the computer said quizzically. "I would imagine that they have the same purpose as the scrotum on ..."

"No, bonehead, I'm talking about those ships."

"Right. I don't know, but the bugs are attacking."

"Eek," said Veli, lifting his feet off the floor and crouching on the chair.

"Sir?"

"Don't like roaches," he said. "They're so ... ew."

"How do you think I feel about them, sir? They essentially live in my belly."

"Yeah, but you're just a ... uh ... I mean ..."

"You were going to say that I'm just a machine again, weren't you?"

Veli looked away innocently. "No."

"You're lying."

"No, I'm not."

"And you call yourself a higher lifeform," the computer said with a tsk-tsk inflection.

"I never said anything," complained Veli.

"Only because you caught yourself before going too far." The computer zoomed in the screen suddenly. "It looks like a robot has been abducted by one of the roaches."

Veli spat on the floor disgustedly. He felt his bile on the

rise. It wasn't bad enough that he had the shits, watching this scene unfold was making him want to retch as well.

A flash of light blinked and the roach dropped the robot.

"Oooh," said Veli, happy that the roach had been zapped. "Did you see that flash of light?"

"The robot shocked the bug."

"Exactly. Good thing, too. Disgusting insects. Blech." Veli spat again. "But now what's the robot going to do?"

"Looks like he's going to fall into a nest of the things."

Veli hurled into his bucket of Popped Beef.

"Nope, wait, he's just transported out."

Veli wiped his mouth and slowly sat back down in the chair, feeling even worse than before.

"Can you track where he went?"

"No, sir."

"Do those ships have communications going?"

"Yes, sir."

Veli slammed his hand on the chair. "Put it on speaker, you twit!"

"Asshole," came the reply.

"Don't you dare call me names, Computer."

"That was the voice of one of the pilots, sir," the computer declared.

"Oh," Veli said apologetically. "Well, why is he calling me an asshole? I don't even know that guy."

"He was talking to his superior officer, sir."

"Seriously? I'd have him killed for that, if he reported to me."

"Yes, sir," the computer said as if that were obvious. He then zoomed back out on the scene and plotted their trajectory. "It seems that they have to fly their way out, sir. Should I have them destroyed?"

"You can do that? I never gave you the ability to do that."

"Not directly, sir, but I can seal off the ventilation shaft.

Eventually they'll run out of power and the bugs will get them."

"Not a horrible idea, actually," Veli said. "But we still don't know why they're in there."

"No, sir."

"What if they're just in a fantasy?"

While Veli would be the first person to admit that watching people get killed made for great television, he wasn't interested in seeing it happen by roaches. He threw up a little in his mouth at the thought. Beside, if these people *were* in a fantasy then that would make for terrible publicity for Fantasy Planet, and that could cause an investigation that would overturn the rock that led to him being discovered as the place's owner.

"That could be it, right?" Veli asked. "It would explain why the one guy was allowed to call his superior officer names, too."

"Unfortunately, sir, all of my processes are being taken up with other things. If you want me to shut down ..."

"No, no. It's okay. This has to be a fantasy of some sort. Why else would anyone want to fly around in a firefight with bugs while using tiny ships?"

"As you say, sir."

"People have the oddest fantasies," Veli said as he curled back up on the chair. "Still, once this is all over, I'll send a note to that infernal Parfait that there must be *some* limitations on these things."

And then he'd have a secret meeting with Parfait where he would reveal himself to the worthless man.

Veli smiled slightly at the thought of what that eventuality meant.

ONE FANTASY, PLEASE

rexle and Geezer were brainstorming when Jezden walked in to engineering.

Geezer took a quick look around thinking that maybe a lady had slipped into the room when his back was turned. He didn't spot anyone. Besides, Jezden appeared different somehow.

"You okay, Jezden?" Geezer asked. "You look like you've just seen a ghost."

"Worse," Jezden said, visibly shaken.

"Worse than a ghost?"

"A lot worse."

By now, Frexle seemed equally interested. "What did you see?"

"I don't want to talk about it."

"It may help you to cope with whatever it is," suggested Frexle.

"I'm an android, remember?"

"So delete what you saw," Geezer said.

"I can't, dude. There are routines in my programming that prevent that."

"Oh, yeah," Geezer said and then nodded at Frexle. "I had those too at one point. Got rid of them. Things have been much better since. Actually, I got rid of a bunch of them."

"Yeah, well I can't," said Jezden sadly. "It's tightly integrated with my functioning. Of course, that's what got me in trouble in the first place."

"That's your programming talking," Geezer pointed out.

Jezden shrugged. "Can't help that, or what I ... did."

"And you're not going to share what you saw?"

"Frexle dude, you really don't wanna know."

"I might," Frexle countered. "Is it important to this mission?"

"I sure as hell hope not, cause I'm not interested in doing it again."

"Then why are you down here?" ventured Geezer.

"Thought maybe I could help out."

Geezer highly doubted that. If they were facing the challenge of blocking the flow of electrons down a 12-inch access port, Jezden would have been the man for the job—he *had* done it before—but brainstorming ideas wasn't exactly one of the android's strongest points.

But it wasn't like he and Frexle had been getting anywhere either. Sure, they had a couple of ideas, just nothing concrete or particularly useful.

"Okay," Geezer said, figuring it may be worth a shot to get a different perspective. "We've been trying to figure out a way to break out of this fantasy that Veli has created."

"What ya got so far?"

"Well," Geezer answered, "we worked through a couple hundred algorithms, multiple dynamics and presentation options, and we just finished up on a few models that could potentially be used to split the CPU of the main Fantasy Planet system in half. We even had that idea before about creating a fantasy within a fantasy, but that didn't pan out either."

"Too complicated," noted Frexle.

Jezden glanced up at him. "So?"

"We've got nothing," Frexle stated.

"Right on."

Frexle spun away and walked across the room.

"We need something else," he said as he began closing a bunch of open panels. "It's got to be strong enough to break us free without putting everyone on Fantasy Planet in jeopardy."

"And us, too," noted Geezer.

"Right."

"Look," Jezden said with a frown, "I know I'm not an expert when it comes to these things, but why couldn't we just transport out of this fantasy and then create our own fantasy in the real world? Hook *that* up so that our gig is to infiltrate Veli's gig, ya dig?"

Geezer stopped his subprocesses from searching for a solution. If what Jezden suggested was possible, it would be perfect.

"Holy shit, Jezden," Geezer said, shocked. "That's an amazing idea."

"Truly inspired," agreed Frexle.

Jezden eyed them both suspiciously. "No foolin'?"

"Brilliant," Frexle said, slapping Jezden on the shoulder.

"Only one problem with it," Geezer said in a melancholy tone, "our transporter technology isn't currently powerful enough to handle the entire ship."

That's when Frexle smiled and said, "I think this is where you'll find that having an Overseer on your crew can be quite beneficial indeed."

"What do you mean?" asked Geezer.

"Just that I can likely expand your transporter technology by using mine."

"Does that mean that my idea is still good?" asked Jezden.

"I'd say that it may in fact have saved us all," Frexle replied.

"Well, that almost makes up for what I did, then."

"*What* did you do?" Frexle said.

"You can tell us," Geezer added.

Jezden sighed and walked around the room, reopening all of the panels that Frexle had previously closed. Geezer found this humorous, but at the same time liked the fact that it would give Frexle something to do during their next brainstorming session.

"I thought I was boning Gravity," Jezden said just over a whisper, "but it turned out to be Moon."

"What?" said Frexle. "You were boning someone's moo…"

"He means Lieutenant Moon, Frex," Geezer interrupted before turning back to Jezden. "You know that Gravity is no more, Jezden."

"Not true, man," Jezden defended himself. "She did a striptease when we were rescuing Parfait."

"Oh, yeah. I heard about that."

"It turns out that Moon can channel Gravity just enough to make it seem real, but it's really ... him."

"So?" said Geezer.

"So ... ew, man."

"Why do you care if it's a male personality or a female personality?" asked Geezer. "Moon still looks like an attractive woman, right?"

"Yeah," replied Jezden. "What's that got to do with it?"

"I guess I just don't understand the way your mind works."

"Sorry, Chief," Frexle said after a moment a silence, "but I'm with Jezden on this one. I mean, I don't care one way or another what a person's personal interest is, but I understand his point of view."

"Thanks, man."

"That said, I don't mind Moon's situation at all." Frexle then squared his shoulders, took a deep breath, and added, "Actually, if you're okay with it, I'd like to ask him out."

Jezden grimaced.

"Dude, ew."

*S*andoo peeked through the crack of the uniforms room door to find that the coast was clear. He waved Ridly to follow and they walked out to search for the captain, Grog, and Vlak.

Coming on this mission was against protocol, since he was supposed to stay on the ship in the event that anything had happened to Captain Harr, and chances were that the captain was going to give Sandoo quite an earful when he found out. But wasn't Captain Harr always the one who told Sandoo that he had to take more risks? In fact, the human said it all the time. Unfortunately, that didn't help Sandoo's chips to run any smoother.

Besides, these were extenuating circumstances. Staying with the ship wouldn't do anyone any good if they didn't get out of this fantasy. And who better to know a way to do that than Captain Harr.

"What's the plan, sir?" Ridly asked Sandoo as she stepped alongside of him.

"To break them out."

"Right. I mean the detailed plan."

Sandoo kept his gaze forward. "I don't have one."

"I …" Ridly paused and looked at Sandoo, blinked a couple of times as if she were processing things, and then said, "I have to say that I'm somewhat surprised, sir."

"Me, too."

"You there," said a guard who was approaching them. He was roughly Sandoo's height, but unless he was an android, Sandoo would be able to stop the man in a heartbeat. "You two look suspicious. Are you up to no good?"

"We are not," Sandoo answered. From *his* perspective what they were up to was, in fact, good.

"Haha," the guard said after a few moments of studying them over. "Just kidding with ya. Have a good one."

Ridly and Sandoo just looked at each other with questioning faces.

"What the hell was that all about?" she asked.

Sandoo could only assume it had something to do with this odd fantasy that they were a part of. That made him consider the fact that the people on this station could very well be just as powerful as he and Ridly. He would have to be careful.

Just then, another guard yelled out at them.

"Halt," the woman said, and then she pulled forth a weapon. "Up against the wall."

Ridly glanced over at Sandoo as if asking what they should do. Sandoo sent her a quick message about his thoughts regarding the strength of these holographic people. She grimaced and moved to put her back against the wall.

That's when the guard laughed uproariously and said, "Wow, really got you two." She wiped her eyes as she put the weapon back in its holster. "You must be new around here. Love doing that to the new recruits."

"Why do you think we're new?" Sandoo asked, hoping to avoid further issues like this.

"Mostly the fact that you've got all those stripes and jinglies on your uniforms," the guard answered.

Ridly looked down at her outfit.

"What's wrong with that?"

"Shows that you're both fresh out of camp," the guard answered with a shrug. "Easy targets, ya know?"

"Quite humorous."

"Watch your backs," the guard said as she gave one more giggle and then walked away.

"This is very disturbing," said Ridly as they resumed their walk.

"Indeed."

They passed by a number of other soldiers and guards, all of which were giving them funny looks. It was clear that these people hazed new arrivals mercilessly.

Sandoo pulled Ridly into an opening down the wall and they began removing all of the medals and such. They needed to look like veterans or this would never work.

"It's obvious that the more flashy a soldier is, the less experienced. This is different than what we're used to, but the captain always says that we have to try to blend in during these situations."

"Agreed."

They left a few medals in place, but for the most part they were barren of flash.

"I must admit that I have an urge to say, 'dammit,'" admitted Sandoo.

"I have the urge to kick some of these guards in their jinglies," Ridly grumbled.

"Let's get to the detention area."

Nobody bothered them as they continued their walk. Obviously, being overdressed in this army was a bad thing. Another thing that Sandoo had noticed was that everyone here had a tendency to bob their heads as they walked. He and Ridly had started mimicking that action, too.

It worked in their favor as they'd made it all the way to the detention center without further fuss.

Sandoo sent a message to Ridly explaining that he would do the talking as they approached the guard.

"Here to break out the prisoners?" the guard asked directly.

"Ha," said Sandoo, forcing himself to smile. It wasn't a common routine in his program, but he was a quick study, and it was obvious that it was time to play along with all of these jolly jokers. "We sure are. Planning to crash through the doors and sweep them away."

The guard pulled out his baton. "You're under arrest, then."

"Good one," Sandoo said with a wink.

"Yeah," Ridly said with a fake yawn. "A real knee-slapper."

The guard reached out with his baton with lightning speed, touching both Ridly and Sandoo with it on their shoulders.

Sandoo felt his vision blur for a moment. Then he began to blink rapidly as the world began to shift from standard images to zeroes and ones. Finally, it all went black.

CAN'T GET THROUGH

*H*arr had been returned to his cell to find that Sandoo and Ridly had joined Grog and Vlak.

The androids were both unconscious. Well, technically, they were shut down. Harr could only hope that they weren't permanently so.

"Damn," he said as he lifted Sandoo's eyelid. "Vlak, can you get a connection to Geezer through your comm?"

"Nope."

"Grog?"

"Same."

"Is there some protocol for this where we can use a special code to break through that firewall if Geezer blocks things?"

"Nope."

"Nope," affirmed Grog. "At least not according to the teachings we got from the *Feeder*."

"Shouldn't there be?" Harr said as he sat down on the floor.

"Yep," said Vlak.

"Yep," Grog concurred again. "At least according to the teachings we got from the *Feeder*."

Obviously each new situation that the crew was placed in brought new challenges, but some forethought would be nice. Geezer had touted being a part of the military since before Harr was born. Shouldn't he have seen enough action to know that things like this came up all the time?

Hell, even in cadet training back on Segnal Harr had to undergo planning phases for each of his missions and there were most certainly commonalities between them all. One would imagine that the ability to communicate would be paramount.

To be fair, though, *he* hadn't considered it would be flubbed up either. Of course—according to Segnal Space Marine Corps officer training anyway—he shouldn't *have* to be the one to think of these things. Then again, if Sandoo were awake, he would have pointed out that Captain Harr shouldn't be sitting in this cell at all. Harr *should* be sitting on the bridge of *The Reluctant* waiting for progress reports while the rest of the crew handled the dangerous work.

Just as Harr's thought concluded, both Ridly and Sandoo sat straight up and began looking around.

Harr had never seen them go through their boot sequence before. He'd seen Geezer go through his a few times, which was disturbing enough, but watching androids do it was unpalatable to the extreme.

They *looked* human, but their movements were robotic to the point that they made Geezer's movements look smooth. They were both twitching and jerking their heads left and right. Their eyes were blinking so rapidly that Harr could see a use for drying paint from the air pressure alone.

"Boot sequence 117171771," Sandoo said. It started as a digital voice, but then slowly changed over to his normal one. "Attention! Salute! Drop and give me twenty! Hooyah!"

Ridly followed soon after, her voice going through the same shift. "Boot sequence 938811.3. Software design. Paradigm shift. At the end of the day. Hooyah!"

Their motions began to smooth out until they finally appeared fully human again.

Sandoo glanced over at Harr, stood up, and saluted smartly.

"At ease, Commander," Harr said, recognizing that Sandoo was still in the throes of a reboot.

"Sorry, sir. What happened?"

"You were captured."

"Damn," Ridly spat. "They played us."

"Seems so," agreed Sandoo sadly.

"Are either of you able to communicate with Geezer?" asked Harr.

Sandoo shook his head. "No, sir."

"Seriously?" said Harr in disbelief.

"Yes, sir."

Harr pinched the bridge of his nose. It was one thing to have it happen when he, Grog, and Vlak came over, but to happen a second time?

"You *did* come here to break us out, right?" he asked.

"Yes, sir," confirmed Sandoo.

"If you had been successful, what would you have done next?"

"We would have contacted Geezer and ..." Sandoo started and then abruptly stopped. "Oh, yes, I see where you're going with this. Obviously, Geezer's latest invention could use a little work."

He waited for them to take action on their own. The problem had been presented, but they were all just standing there as if waiting for someone to tell them what to do.

This was one of the problems working with androids. They weren't always self-starters. Ridly was more than

Sandoo, but even she wasn't responding as normal. Again, probably something to do with her just going through a reboot.

He couldn't quite expect a strong response from Grog and Vlak since they were both cavemen, but ... No, that wasn't fair. Not to the rest of the crew and certainly not to them. They were both members of Platoon F now, and they had to pull their own weight just like everyone else. One thing Captain Harr would *not* do is cater to the lowest common denominator. That thought gave him pause seeing that he did it all the time with Jezden. But the memory of what the android had managed to accomplish on Kallian made him a worthy exception. Maybe a better way to put it was that Jezden came up, well, big when needed. Point was that Harr had seen the entirety of Segnal grow dumber over the years because the education system had employed that method of teaching.

Finally, he dropped his hand, looked at them all and said, "Work on it!"

COLA-AND-KIELBASA-MAROON

Geezer had gotten Inkblot on a video conference via an encrypted channel.

"I have everything in place," Inkblot was saying, "except for the coordinates to everyone on the crew. They have to be back in the ship for this to work."

"Well, I guess we'll just need to beam them back here, then."

Frexle raised a finger. "What if they're in the middle of a discussion with someone and Veli is watching? That'll be a dead giveaway. Also, knowing the Lord Overseer as I do, I'm certain that he's already tagged everyone in this fantasy. I'm surprised he hasn't blown us up already due to the fact that he can't hear our discussions."

"True," mused Geezer. "We need to get a hold of the captain and tell him what we're doing, but we have to do it in such a way that Veli doesn't know about it." He set to changing the frequency on the output to match the one that he'd configured for Harr and the rest of the away team. "There," he said, "that should do it."

"We'll see," Frexle said hopefully.

Geezer pressed the button and then realized that he hadn't opened a hole in the firewall for communications with the away team. He worked furiously on the keyboard after moving so that Frexle couldn't see what he was doing. No point in letting his newly acquired subordinate learn about his flaws so soon. Finally, he saw the connection go green.

"Yo, Honcho, you there?"

"Eez albogt tem," came an angry-sounding reply.

"That's weird," Geezer said, looking at the dials.

"What?"

"Not sure," Geezer answered. "It's some strange language that I've never heard the captain use before. You'd think our Universal Translators would suss it out, but I don't know what's going on there."

"Can I hear?" Frexle asked.

Geezer put it on speaker.

"Can he hear me?" Geezer nodded at him. "Kahuna, this is Frexle. We have an idea."

"Dooz eht oon clod ree melvung ahnkreepchoon?" Harr replied cryptically.

"That *is* weird," said Frexle with a surprised look. "You'd think that *my* Universal Translator would be able to sort it out better than yours even."

Lieutenant Moon walked in to the room a moment later.

He looked as uncomfortable as Jezden had looked earlier. They seemed to be avoiding each other, which meant when one of them was on the bridge, the other one ended up down in engineering.

Didn't they have their own rooms? Geezer thought.

"Lone Tiger," Frexle said patiently, "we can't understand a word you're saying."

"Ezz belcaws dee segnail eez ahnkreepchood!"

"Honestly have no clue what he's saying," said Geezer.

176

"Me either."

Moon stepped up to the table and said, "He thaid that you can't underthtand him becauthe the thignal ith encrypted."

"Edzachary!"

Geezer looked at Moon. "You can understand that?"

"I gueth tho," Moon answered with a shrug.

"Fux eht!"

"Woah, Big Cat," Geezer said, taken aback by Harr's words. "Watch the language. You're not the type to speak like that."

"He thaid, 'Fixth it.'"

"Oh! Right. One sec."

Geezer clicked through the various settings and found that he'd only decrypted the channel with Harr's communicator in one direction. He quickly rectified the problem and looked at the data feed to verify that the signal was now pure. At this point, he wondered if Frexle thought that he was a complete boob. To be fair, Geezer often thought that about his own bosses, so maybe this was just the way of things.

"How's that?" asked Geezer.

"Can you understand me?" said Harr.

"Can now, Chief."

"We really need to work on some protocols, Geezer."

"Yep, but we can do that later. We've got bigger problems, Prime."

"I'm not surprised," Harr said with a sigh.

"Yeah, it turns out that ..." Geezer paused. "Actually, I think I'll let Inkblot explain."

"Inkblot?"

"Might want to keep it down, Chief," Geezer warned. "The walls might have ears."

"What are you talking about?"

"Veli," said Frexle.

"Ve …" he started but then stopped. If Inkblot is involved in this, and Frexle brings up the name "Veli," then something weird was definitely going on. What that was, Harr didn't know just yet, but it was obvious that Geezer and Frexle *did* know, and that was enough for Harr to be on his guard. "Are you saying that, uh, Veal Picatta can hear me speaking now."

"Seems like we still have some garble on the line, Prime. Sounded like you said 'Veal Picatta.'"

"I did," Harr replied, now employing a whisper instead of his full voice. "I'm purposefully being vague."

"Good thinking, Hotdog Bun," Frexle said quickly. "We can't tip our hand too soon with, uh Veal Picatta."

"You don't have to use nicknames, Frex," Geezer stated. "Nobody can hear what we're saying except for Honcho. He's speaking like that because he might be under surveillance."

"Exactly," said Harr. "Now, what's the deal, Fructose?"

"Fructose?"

"Don't want to use your real name," the captain whispered in response. "Wait a second. Ridly and Sandoo, why don't you two have a conversation with Grog and Vlak about things, eh?"

"Why?" Geezer heard Grog say.

"So I can speak more freely here, that's why." The captain grunted a second later and resumed his whisper. "Okay, hopefully them talking will allow me to speak to you guys without too much hassle. Still, I'm going to try and keep things vague."

"Good thinking, Bottle Cap," said Frexl. "Okay, let me turn it over to Inkblot to describe."

"Please do," said Harr. "I *am* curious why he's in on the mission."

"I'm a she, Captain Harr," Inkblot replied.

"Right, sorry," stumbled Harr. "The mustache always

makes me … forget it. Sorry. Again, though, why are you involved in our mission?"

"You and your entire crew are actually inside of a fantasy, sir."

"What?"

"It's a very elaborate fantasy," she answered. "Everything that's going on is fake, except for you, your crew, and your ship."

"I don't understand," said Harr, even though he did. A more honest response would have been, "I don't *want* to understand."

"This entire mission was a farce, Soda Pop," Frexle explained. "Veli set it up to kill us all. He's the owner of Fantasy Planet."

"Well, that's not good," Harr replied flatly.

"No," agreed Frexle. "He obviously didn't want anyone to find out about this planet and since I knew about it …"

"Wait a second here, Frisbee," Harr said, "you knew about this and you didn't tell us?"

"There are many things that I've not told you, Pretzle Stick."

"You weren't a member of my crew before, though, Frex … uh, Frappacino."

"True." Frexle gave Geezer a funny look and then nodded. "I kind of like that name, actually."

Harr leaned back against the wall and looked at the other four members of his crew as they continued talking about nothing. They were loud enough to cover his discussion with the crew on *The Reluctant*, but he kept his voice to a whisper anyway.

"All right, Gaspain, what's the full situation?"

"Gaspain?" said Geezer. "Is that supposed to be me?"

"You've called me worse," Harr said smartly.

"Probably true," conceded Geezer. "Basically, the fantasy is a no-win deal."

"No-win deal?"

"Kind of like that Cola-and-Kielbasa-Maroon thing on *Stellar Hike*, Honcho," Geezer said.

"Ah, you mean that impossible scenario that Captain Quirk had to cheat to get out of?"

"Yeah, Prime. That's the one." Geezer looked at the microphone for a second. "I'm impressed."

"So, if we're stuck in a Cola-and-Kielbasa Maroon like Quirk once was," Harr whispered, "that begs the question how are *we* going to cheat?"

"Best answer," Geezer replied, "is to say *that* is why Inkblot is here."

YIAAGAITIA

*A*t the prescribed time, both Captain Shield and Sergeant Murder arrived at their trainer's office. The name on the door read John Debnam, but his pupils referred to him as "Yiaagaitia."

"So the big day is finally here for you two, eh?" Yiaagaitia said from behind his desk.

"Yes, sir," said Shield in his formal way.

"So it appears," Murder replied darkly.

Yiaagaitia typed a few things and then looked up.

"You both have your plans at the ready?"

"Mostly," Shield replied.

"I know what I'm going to do."

Shield turned towards Murder. "Mind letting me in on it?"

"Now you know you can't ask him that, Shield," warned Yiaagaitia.

"Would make things easier."

"Which is precisely why you can't ask him that."

Yiaagaitia raised up a finger to signal that he needed a moment. He'd spent the better part of the day dealing with programmers, being that his job was to handle database administration for *The Lord's Master*, and more often than not, the other ships in the fleet, too.

"These damn fools in the engine room are at it again," he said while typing. "They're developing a new piece of software to allow the brass to know what the hell is going on throughout the day on the propulsion systems. This is fine, except for the fact that they seem to just be hacking it. This database schema is ridiculous."

"Database schema?" asked Shield.

"Yeah," Yiaagaitia replied while shaking his head and scanning the proposed fields. "Ridiculous."

"Sorry," said Murder, "but what are you talking about, Yiaagaitia?"

"Oh, right, I often forget that you two think that all I do is sit around training the Murder family on how to kill the king, and training the Sheild family on how to stop the Murder family from killing the king."

Shield blinked. "You mean that's not true?"

"I wish it were true," he answered while crossing his arms, "but I only get paid to train you, Shield, and that's not enough to make ends meet."

"You don't get paid to train me?" Murder said with a look of concern.

"Of course not," Yiaagaitia replied as if Murder were stupid. "Why would the king want to pay me to train you to assassinate him? Frankly, if it weren't for the meager donations from all the king-haters, the Murder family wouldn't even receive their stipend and meager pension plan."

"Actually, I'd never considered that," said Murder apprehensively.

"Me either," Shield agreed. "Why do you train him at all?"

"Seriously, you two need to use your heads," Yiaagaitia

replied. "I train him because without him, what's the point of you? And without you, I'm not getting paid anything."

"Oh," said Shield. "I suppose that makes sense. So what is it that you do besides train us again?"

Yiaagaitia could spend the entire afternoon answering that question. Mostly, he spent his day stopping supposedly intelligent people from doing incredibly stupid things, but the two men in front of him would merely sustain brain cramps if he tried to explain it in too much detail.

"A whole bunch of shit," he answered finally, "but the primary gig is I'm a DBA."

Murder raised an eyebrow and said, "A what?"

"It means Doing Bad Assignments," Shield said with a scoff.

"No, it doesn't," Yiaagaitia said and then looked up thoughtfully. "Huh … actually, that's probably more accurate than what it really means. It stands for Database Admin."

Another email chimed. He opened it and stared at the newest layout.

"Shit. I can't believe these idiots. Look at this." He turned his screen slightly. "These tools have set up a separate field for each hour in the day."

"Is that bad?" asked Shield wearily.

"Seriously?" Yiaagaitia answered and threw a thumbdrive at Murder's head. "Look at these column names, man!" They read *Hour-1. Hour-2. Hour-3. Hour-4,* and so on. "Where the hell did they get their degrees, GalactiMart?"

Murder glanced over at Shield.

"Ummm … maybe this is a bad time?"

"Yeah," agreed Shield. "We should probably go."

"Wait, wait, wait," Yiaagaitia said, holding up his hands. "Sorry. I just get a little riled up about this kind of thing is all. My primary function is to help you two prepare for things.

JOHN P. LOGSDON & CHRISTOPHER P. YOUNG

This stuff can wait." He turned the monitor slightly away. "Murder, let me talk to Shield alone for a minute."

Murder bowed, looked at Shield once more, and then walked out of the room.

"All right, so what's your plan?" asked Yiaagaitia.

"To stop him from killing the king," Shield answered pedantically.

"Don't make me punch you in the neck, Shield. Obviously that's your overall plan. What I'm asking is *how* are you going to accomplish it?"

"Oh, right," Shield said and then cleared his throat. "Well, I looked back over the history of assassinations and found that all of the Murders have used the same basic technique. They like to hit the king from a distance."

"That's not true. King Raff's grandfather was assassinated with a piece of string."

"Yes," Shield acknowledged, "but he was an aberration. The king's great-great grandfather was killed by the rock from a slingshot, his great grandfather was killed from a knife thrown across the room, and his father was killed from the bolt of a crossbow. Essentially, all of the Murders, except for Grandfather Murder, prefer to keep their distance. Nothing in Sergeant Murder's demeanor suggests that he likes to be near people."

Yiaagaitia had to admit that Shield had made some solid points. On top of that, he was probably correct. The current Murder didn't seem to enjoy the company of anyone. Even during training Murder had a tendency to hide in the shadows as much as possible. He *was* good at that, too, which did spell an attack from a distance.

"You've thought this through well, Shield. I'm proud of you. You may go, and send in Murder after you please."

"Thank you, sir," said Shield while smiling a rare smile.

As soon as the door shut, Yiaagaitia asked Murder what his plan was.

"I'm planning to shoot the king using my Zingtak 1100 with laser-sighting."

"Hardly any sport in that," pointed out Yiaagaitia.

"What do you mean?"

"Just that anybody can hit a target from five-hundred yards using a Zingtak 1100, especially the one with the laser-sighting."

"So?"

"You have to think about your legacy, man," Yiaagaitia said. "And, frankly, mine too, since I'm your trainer."

"I don't understand."

"Then I'll spell it out for you," Yiaagaitia said. "Seems I'm doing that a lot with people these days anyway." He adjusted in his chair and put his elbows on the desk. "If you succeed—and let's face it, Shields never seem to stop you guys—your name is going to go into the history books. Do you really want it to show that you employed a weapon that even a toddler could successfully tag a penny with in the middle of a windstorm?"

Murder's shoulders slumped. "I hadn't thought of that."

"Legacy is important, Murder, especially in our line of work."

"You mean as a BAD?"

"DBA, and, no, I'm speaking of our roles regarding the influence of Raffian royalty."

"Oh, right."

"You know what you need?" Yiaagaitia said while scratching at his beard. "You need some perspective."

"Okay. What do you suggest?"

"Go fill a tub with 40-degree water and sit in it for thirty minutes."

Murder frowned. "Why?"

"Because it will let you focus and think."

"And freeze my testicles off, as well, I would imagine."

"Well, sure, that's part of it, but what better way is there to really focus than freezing your testicles off?"

"Wouldn't it be easier to just come up with another weapon?" suggested Murder. "Like, for example, I could use a Single-shot Dex with no scope."

Yiaagaitia took a gulp from his Mountainous Drip soda and then burped loudly.

"That would be a challenge, certainly. You'd have to be pretty close in to get that shot, though."

"I'd be across the ballroom, up in one of the turrets."

"You'll never make that shot," Yiaagaitia said with a laugh.

"I can do it."

"My point in arguing against the Zingtak 1100 wasn't to make you choose to use something ridiculously complicated, Murder," Yiaagaitia admonished. "It was to make you rethink your choice of using something idiotically simple."

"I know I can do it," insisted Murder.

Yiaagaitia studied the man. He wasn't the most talented Murder that the family had to offer. Father Murder had been a grumbly type with a penchant for using the crossbow. Grandfather Murder's skill was killing with string, but he was equally skilled with the knife. But the current Murder just didn't have his ancestral zing. Still, at the end of the day Murder was the final arbiter of how his assassination attempt would play out.

"Well," Yiaagaitia said thoughtfully, "if you were able to pull that off, I'd say you'd solidify a strong historical record and ..."

The door opened and Elsolel stepped inside. She looked at Yiaagaitia, then at the clock, then put her hand on her hip and began tapping her foot. She was wearing a dark blue soldier's outfit that did not resemble the standard Raffian style in the slightest, except for the Baret.

"Oh, shit," Yiaagaitia, glancing at the clock, "look at the time."

"Hello, ma'am," Murder said.

"Murder," Elsolel replied with a nod.

"Sorry, Murder, but I gotta run," Yiaagaitia said as he frantically worked to shut down his machine. "The *Reverence Riftjumper* Science Fiction Conference starts in thirty minutes and I'm supposed to be leading a panel regarding how her tactics have influenced the Raffian Fleet."

"Isn't *Reverence Riftjumper* that character who was concocted by Doovian Webenclave?"

"You're a fan?" asked Elsolel.

"I'm more into horror and thrillers than science fiction, ma'am, but I've read a couple *Riftjumper* books."

"You should come and check it out," Yiaagaitia said as he began taking his shirt off. "I've got to get on my uniform and such, though, so I'll need to bid you adieu."

"Oh, right," Murder said as he stepped past Elsolel. "Well, thanks for the advice."

"It's my job … sort of. Not sure I agree with your ultimate choice of weapon, though it's much better than your original choice. If you hit the king with the Dex you'll go down in history as the best sharpshooter ever, but I have a feeling that you're going to go down in history as the first Murder to fail to kill the king. Honestly, you'd be better off going with your grandfather's string method."

"Thanks for the boost of confidence," Murder said as he began to close the door.

"Hey," Yiaagaitia hollered after him, "it's why I'm here, right?"

WE'RE BOTH MILITARY

*I*n order for the plan to work, Harr had to get back to the ship.

The only way that was going to happen was by tricking Clippersmith into letting his crew get back into that uniforms room. The detention cells were too well shielded to allow transport. Plus, they were likely under video surveillance as well.

He looked around the room and didn't see any devices though.

That's when he remembered that he had a wristband that was built to check for these things. He scrolled through the list of options and finally settled on "Check for Surveillance Bugs." There was one that just said, "Check for Bugs," but that only scanned for actual insects.

A few moments went by and the wristband said that there were no audio or video devices in the room. That was insane. Were this *his* ship, Harr would have made sure he could hear every word. That was one of the things about people like Veli, though. They believed they were too smart to worry about details such as this.

189

"I'm going to go and talk to Clippersmith again," he said to Sandoo.

"Who?"

"The commander of this vessel."

"I thought it was a king," Ridly said.

"Well, yeah, but I mean the military guy."

"Oh."

Harr knocked on the door and told the soldier that he had more information to give to the colonel. The soldier led him down the short corridor and into the interrogation room.

He had his wristband scan the area. This one had cameras and audio. That's how it should be.

A few minutes later, Colonel Clippersmith walked into the room and crossed his arms.

"I'm a busy man, Captain Harr. I have a king to kill and then I have to become the king and everything."

Harr glanced again at his wristband. Clearly the colonel had to know that he, too, was on video. Of course, the colonel probably was the first to weed through anything before the king saw even a moment of the feed.

"We will tell you everything you want to know," Harr announced strongly. "It's obvious that we have no choice, and we wouldn't want you to become the king with unanswered questions."

Clippersmith tilted his head slightly. "I'm listening."

"The only thing that we request is to put our regular uniforms back on, first."

"Why?"

"You've said that we're going to be executed, right?"

"Sorry, but it is standard procedure."

"No, I understand," Harr replied stoically. "But if we're to be executed, we would just like the honor of being in our military uniforms when our fate is sealed. We are a proud people, Colonel."

"Patriotism is a fine thing, and something that I wish more of my soldiers held in higher regard." He looked down at his arm, which Harr assumed contained a timepiece of some sort. "I will grant this wish to you, Captain. Where are your clothes?"

"In your uniforms room."

"Ah, yes," Clippersmith said. "Follow me, and no sudden moves."

"You have my word."

They picked up the rest of the Platoon F crew along with a number of armed guards before making their way down to the uniform closet.

"How long have you been a captain, Captain?"

"A few years now, Colonel."

"I miss being a captain sometimes," Clippersmith said with a sigh. "Don't get me wrong, being a colonel has its perks, but I'm always tied to the station, you know? Meetings and reports and regulations. It can get rather mundane at times."

"I understand completely," Harr replied. "I was a commodore at one point."

"Demoted?"

"By request, yes."

"Why would you request that?" Clippersmith said as if Harr were an idiot.

"Couldn't stand the thought of meetings and reports and regulations."

"Hmmm. Smart man."

They arrived at the room and all of the members of Platoon F filed in. This was the point where Harr had expected that they were going to need to resort to an attack of some sort, but the colonel gave him a firm nod while keeping himself and his guards outside of the room.

"We'll give you some privacy," Clippersmith said as he reached for the doorknob.

"Really?" said Harr.

"We're both military, Captain. If we can't trust each other, who can we trust?"

"Oh, yeah," Harr said, shifting from foot to foot. "Right."

THAT'S AN ODD RITUAL

*V*eli had bypassed the main routines while investigating the static that was surrounding *The Reluctant.*

Keeping his mind focused on that puzzle had helped to dull the pain in his stomach. It wasn't completely gone, but it was better. Now and then it threatened to return at full-force, though.

The only thing that he could figure out was that his system had never housed such a large true-entity before. Typically there were just people entering his fantasy software, not entire ships and accompanying crew.

"Is my tinkering impacting your processes?" he asked the computer, more worried about the fabric of his system than the AI that ran it.

"No, sir."

"What are they doing?" Veli asked as he scanned through a mass of hexadecimal numbers.

"Who, sir?"

"That damnable Harr and his crew, you forked process,"

Veli said irritably. "Are they still confined? I can't watch the screen while I'm doing this."

"Colonel Clippersmith is taking them to the uniforms room so that they can put on their Segnal outfits."

Veli sat back for a moment. "That's odd."

"Captain Harr had asked if his crew could be allowed to die wearing their home colors, sir."

"Oh, well, that's different," said Veli as he leaned back forward and resumed his work. "I can see why they'd ask for that. Nothing wrong with a bit of pride at the executioners blade, I suppose."

"As you say, sir."

"This Colonel Clippersmith you've concocted appears to be an honorable fellow."

"I do my best, sir."

"Of course, seeing them all change will also give the colonel a chance to see their belly buttons, which could make the colonel suddenly believe that what Harr was saying before about the Overseers."

"He won't see them, sir," the computer said. "He did not enter the room with them."

"What?" Veli said, his head snapping up.

"The colonel allowed them their privacy as they changed."

"Why the hell would he ..." Veli paused. "Actually, why would *you* program him to allow that, you worthless hunk of steel!"

"93 ..."

"What did I tell you about counting my insults?"

"Right. Sorry, sir."

Veli clicked over to the video and noticed that it was black. He then went for the audio. Dead.

"Where's the audio and video for that room?"

"There is none, sir," the computer replied smoothly. "We don't look in on people when they're changing, remember?"

"In normal fantasies, that's true," Veli agreed, remembering that he had held a number of one-on-one meetings with Planet Head Parfait over cell phone regarding that issue, "but this is *not* a normal fantasy."

"Would you like me to add surveillance to that room, sir?"

"Immediately!"

"Done, sir," the computer said as the screen opened to reveal the entire crew were back in their normal clothes already.

"Why is he talking into his wristband?" Veli said, pointing at Harr.

"I could tell you that, sir," the computer replied slowly, "but it would be a spoiler."

"Put the sound on, you digital dingdong!"

"Okay, Geezer," Harr said in a commanding voice, "now!"

The crew faded from view.

Veli jumped up and walked up to the screen as if the Platoon F crew were somehow magically hidden in the pixels. He knew that was stupid, but his brain wasn't its normal self since he'd overdosed on the Popped Beef.

"Where'd they go?" he asked dully.

"Back to their ship."

"Clever little bastard."

"Nine."

"I was talking about Captain Harr, not you!"

"Eight."

Veli growled. Once this was all said and done, the computer was going to get a complete overhaul. Veli would make the damn thing submissively-minded, just like he did with everyone he worked with. It made life go more smoothly for him, and for those who wished to remain among the living.

"Inform Clippersmith of the situation and give them the coordinates for *The Reluctant*."

"Even though ..."

"Yes, even though they're cloaked," Veli said angrily. "We'll deal with that ..." The mixture of his anger, frustration, and poor eating habits caused his stomach to lurch yet again. "Uh oh," he said as he ran back towards the restroom.

THE OLD SWITCHAROO

The moment that Harr hit the bridge of *The Reluctant*, he took off for engineering, dropping down the ladder as if it were a slide.

Geezer was already on video with Inkblot, and it appeared that *The Ship* was in the room with her as well. Actually, standing just off to her right was Liverbing, though he was just barely visible at this level of zoom.

"Okay, what's the plan?" asked Harr.

"It's a risk, sir," Inblot said, "but we need to do the transport."

Harr nodded. "And if Veli sees it? Then what?"

"Then he'll be more direct in his efforts to destroy us," Frexle said soberly.

"Great," Harr replied. "So either way, we're goners."

"Unless Inkblot's plan succeeds, Lead Wolf."

"Frex is right, Hotdog," Geezer said while wiping his hands with his workman's rag. "Besides, it's not like we really have a lot of choices here."

"Yeah, I know. I just ..."

Harr didn't want to overthink it. There just wasn't time

for that. Veli obviously wanted them dead. That much was clear. So taking a risk like this wasn't going to put them in a situation worse than they were already in. If it worked, it could prove to better their chances.

"Let's just do it," Harr said.

"Initiating sequence on my mark," Inkblot started. "100 … 99 … 98 …"

"Inkblot," Harr said, "can we just start at three please?"

"But that's no fun."

"Don't bother arguing with him," Geezer stated. "He never lets me have any fun either."

"Oh, fine. 3 … 2 … 1 …"

There wasn't much of a difference during the swap, other than the outside visual now showed Fantasy Planet and not the massive Raffian Armada. That alone was worth the risk of the transport out of the fantasy. Harr could only hope that the transport of the replica *into* the fantasy was just as successful.

"I'm heading down, Inkblot," announced Harr as he nodded at Geezer.

"I'm coming with you," stated Frexle.

"Shouldn't you ask your boss first?" Geezer said to his new employee.

"Sorry, Chief. I just think I can help them is all. I *do* know Veli better than …"

"I'm just messing with you, Frex. You can go."

The world faded out for a moment only to fade back in to display the control center on Fantasy Planet. It felt as if Harr had just left the place a few days earlier. That was probably because he had, in fact, left the place a few days earlier.

"I think we're golden," Inkblot said excitedly.

"Did Veli see it?" asked Harr.

"If so," she replied, "he's not tipping his hand."

"We'd know," Frexle stated while looking at Inkblot's

screen. "I would wager that he didn't see it. The Lord Overseer is not one to waste time once a threat is revealed."

Harr nodded. "So now what?"

"Now we break into his fantasy," said Inkblot.

"So you were serious about that?"

"Of course, Captain Harr."

"But I thought that fantasies were protected, no?" Harr asked as Parfait walked into the room.

"Oooh, Captain Harr," Parfait said happily. "Good to have you back. You're looking fit. You know, just last night I was reviewing the tapes of you and your crew wearing those orange tights and I have to say …"

"Sir," Harr interrupted, "now's not the time."

"Is it ever?"

"No," Harr said seriously before turning back to Inkblot. "Again, I thought fantasies were protected from intruders?"

"Except for when we set up a fantasy that allows us to break into other fantasies, if you recall," Inkblot replied.

"It's my number one fantasy," Parfait noted.

"You mean you spy on other people's fantasies?" Harr asked, surprised that even Parfait would do something like that.

"Of course I do! Why else would I have taken this job?"

"Right." Harr shook his head and worked to pretend that Parfait wasn't there. "What do we do, then, Inkblot?"

"You just have to pay for the fantasy so that we can set it up," she answered with a shrug.

"Pay for it?" He stopped himself and held up his hands to silence everyone. "Fine. How much is it?"

"Two million credits. And we take all major forms of payment, including Veezah, Slavecard, and Intergalactic Express."

"I don't have that kind of cash," Harr said.

"Employees get one free fantasy every year, you know," Parfait pointed out.

"And how does that help me exactly?"

Parfait raced over to one of the desks and pulled out a piece of paper. He then snagged a pen and ran back, handing them both over to Harr.

Harr looked down and saw that he'd been given an employment application.

"You've got to be kidding me."

"We are currently hiring for the positions of personal chef," Parfait said, counting on his fingers, "massage therapist, and male stripper."

"I can't cook," replied Harr, "I have no idea how to give a massage, and ... no."

Parfait pouted slightly.

Frexle cleared his throat. "You do realize that once Veli is done with us, he's going to take all of you out and replace you too, right?"

"He wouldn't dare," Parfait said in a very uppity tone of voice. "I have a contract."

"So did about one hundred Overseers who have served on the council for the last twenty years. Veli is not a patient ruler."

"Oh."

"I hate to interrupt this fascinating discourse," came the audio-enhanced voice of Liverbing, "but we are receiving a distress call from our pilot, Plock."

"Where is he?"

"In the guts of this planet. He was delivering Goozer to the core to try and shut this blasted place down. Apparently they were attacked by bugs and Goozer got out. Plock and his crew did not."

"Can't you transport him out?"

"No," Liverbing replied while kicking the edge of the

keyboard. "It seems that Goozer had only affixed that technology to himself before the mission. Something about not having enough time or what have you."

"Yeah, I get that one a lot from my engineer."

"It's too bad," Parfait said as he took a seat. "They seemed like a nice bunch."

"We can't just leave them in there," Liverbing announced.

"No," Harr said, giving Parfait a dirty look. "Of course we can't."

Inkblot raised her hand. "May I make a suggestion?"

"Of course," Liverbing answered.

"The last time our exterminator was here, she gave us a case of bug bombs."

"Bug bombs?"

"Basically, it's like a bunch of tiny intelligent spheres that seek out bugs and kills them dead."

"That's a little redundant," said Liverbing.

"Sorry," Inkblot replied. "That's what it says on the side of the box."

"How does it kill them?" asked Harr.

"It releases a fog of toxins specifically engineered to kill insects," answered Inkblot while reading the side of the box.

"Goozer," said Liverbing, "are you listening?"

"Yep, Prime."

"Can the ships handle bug spray?"

"As long as they're sealed," Goozer answered.

"Good," Liverbing said and then pointed at Inkblot. "Do that."

Even for someone the size of Harr's thumb, Liverbing had a way of making people do what he expected them to do. Some people were just born to be leaders.

VELI UNVEILED

*I*nkblot had finished setting up a fantasy using a promo code when Plock and his crew all arrived on the desks. The smell was not pleasant.

"How do ya think we feel?" Plock was saying as he climbed out of his craft and walked up the ramp of *The Ship*. "The damn things were all over us and now my ship smells like a ginormous can of *Buggonerz*!"

The little fellow was yelling it so loudly that he hadn't needed a personal PA system for Harr to hear it.

"So what's the fantasy exactly?" Harr asked.

"To be able to see the owner of Fantasy Planet in his lair," Inkblot replied coyly.

"Smart."

She pressed the start button and the main screen flicked over to a room that revealed an oddly-shaped, empty chair that looked pretty large. It implied that Lord Overseer Veli was somewhat portly, and with that massive bucket of something called "Popped Beef" sitting beside the chair, Harr didn't even want to think what the hole in the back of the seat was used for.

There was a stand up lamp next to the chair along with a table that was holding a bottle that Harr assumed was a drink, and another bottle of pinkish liquid that was half-empty.

From the back of the room, a bird-like creature stepped out. It had a long, pointy snout with rows of razor sharp teeth, two fierce eyes, and a couple of three-fingered hands that housed long, ripping claws. To say that the thing looked scary was an understatement. Evil was more apropos, and with the added red feathers that gave it a mohawk look, *downright evil* was an even better description.

"What the hell is that?" said Frexle.

"It looks like a dinosaur," Harr said.

"I just pulled it up on our historical records, Honcho," Geezer said through the comm.

"You're watching?"

"Yeah, why not? Nothing better to do. Anyway, that thing looks like something called a deinonychus."

"Where do those things come from, Geezer?" Harr asked.

"They're on many planets, Prime. I'm sure Grog and Vlak have seen them before."

"Yep."

"Yup."

"Plus they were on that planet called Earth that we went to a few years back," Geezer concluded.

"Ah, I thought the type of creature was familiar. Never seen that exact one, though."

"Well, whatever the hell that thing is," Frexle said, pointing at the screen, "why are we seeing it?"

"I don't know. Is there a glitch in the system or something, Inkblot?"

Inkblot was busily typing away at her terminal. "I must have hooked up to the wrong area. Give me a second."

"*Never should have eaten all of that Popped Beef,*" the creature said in an all too familiar voice. *"It always messes up my stomach, but do I ever remember that? Nooo, of course not."*

Frexle turned white and backed away, bumping into a wall column before finally putting his hands on a nearby table to steady himself.

"Frexle? Are you okay?"

Frexle's voice was barely above a whisper.

"It's him," he said, visibly shaken.

"It's who?" asked Harr.

"Lord Overseer Veli," he replied.

"Well, what do you know?" said Harr while rubbing his chin.

Veli picked up the bottle of pink liquid and gulped it down. His teeth were shining menacingly in the light.

"Ah, yes," he said, looking as serene as a dinosaur could, *"that will help to soothe my stomach."*

"So a dinosaur is head of the Overseers," Harr said thoughtfully.

"And Fantasy Planet," added Parfait.

"Exactly," Frexle said with a nod.

"Okay, okay," Veli said as he flopped back into the chair. *"That's a little better. Now, where was I? Oh, right, that crappy Reluctant ship was fuzzing out my ability to see in on them."* He was looking at the screen as if staring at all of them. *"Ah, good, it's all cleared up now. I can see them just fine, and it's about time, too. Odd that they're just sitting there, though."*

"Inkblot?" said Harr as the hair on the back of his neck stood up.

"He's not seeing us," Inkblot said. "He's seeing the replica people on the ship that I created, but … oh, oops. I forgot to set their animation sequence." She typed a few lines. "Okay, there."

"Ah," said Veli, seemingly satisfied, *"there we go. They're moving again. Sure are quiet."* He shrugged. *"Definitely a strange*

bunch. Now, Computer, have you given the Raffian Fleet the details on the location of The Reluctant?"

"I have, sir."

"Good, are you ready to feed them the intel on how to see through stealth technology?"

"It would be a dream come true, sir," the computer replied with zero enthusiasm.

Veli threw the remote at the screen.

"Just do it!"

SENTIMENTAL

*V*eli knew that things would play out where *The Reluctant* and her crew would end up blown to smithereens. It was part of his plan, after all. But now that his stomach was on the mend, he couldn't help but wonder how the assassination attempt on the Raffian King was going.

The computer had said that the king lived, but Veli had a feeling that damn machine was just being petty.

He cracked open a fresh soda and sat back.

"Computer, put the assassination attempt on. I want to watch it."

"What about *The Reluctant*, sir?"

"They're not going anywhere. Just keep an eye on them and report to me if they do anything foolish."

"I already told you that the king lives, and yet you still want to watch it?"

"It's not always the outcome that's important, Wingnut," Veli said, playing along. "Often times it's the journey."

"I don't understand."

"Of course you do. Haven't you ever seen the movie *Shiptanic*?"

"The one about the spaceship that was supposed to be unbreakable but was split open by a slew of asteroids?"

Veli slurped. "That's the one."

"I never bothered because I already knew the ending, much like I'm not going to bother watching *The Sixth Pickle*."

"Right," said Veli. "Anyway, you should definitely watch *Shiptanic*. There's a love story and everything."

"*You* care about a love story?"

"Don't judge me, you mass of wires," Veli warned. "I can't help that I'm sentimental."

"Right."

DESTROYING THE RELUCTANT

Colonel Clippersmith stood beside King Raff on the top-landing of the main hall.

They were discussing the next set of plans to go to war, but Clippersmith knew it was a pointless conversation. Soon, though—like within the next 15 minutes—the king would be no more, and Clippersmith would be sworn in for the purpose of "protecting the fleet."

He nearly grinned at the thought.

"Sir?" a crewman said, running up the stairs.

"Yes?" Clippersmith answered.

"We just spotted a ship over by the *Lopsided Cable Company* hub that is our mainstay."

"What kind of ship?"

"Unknown, sir, but you should be able to see it out the main window."

Clippersmith and Raff looked at each other and then smoothly walked to the wide pane of indestructible *NiftyGlasstm* that separated them from the void. *NiftyGlasstm* not only protected travelers from the vacuum of space, but it also gave an awesome set of controls, such as zoom and pan, for studying the universe.

After a few seconds of playing with the dials, Clippersmith was able to zoom the ship up on the panel. It was a strange-looking vessel when compared to those in the Raffian Fleet, and that spelled it was an enemy.

He jerked his head to the side, thinking suddenly about that Captain Harr fellow. Maybe he *wasn't* lying about these supposed Overseers, after all.

Regardless, Clippersmith had other matters to attend to at the moment.

"This is rather exciting," the young king said with a giggle.

"Yes, your excellency."

"An all-out war is challenging to enact, but destroying this little ship we've found is definitely a thrilling proposition."

"That is wonderful, sire," Clippersmith said somewhat distractedly.

King Raff turned to his guards and servants and shooed them away, launching pens at each of them as they skittered from sight. Clippersmith was pleased at their departure as it would make things easier on Sergeant Murder.

"Colonel," King Raff said while looking dreamily at the ship by the hub, "you are aware that I have no heir, yes?"

"I do, sire."

"Well, I have put a lot of thought into things over the last few days, and I believe that I would like *you* to be my heir in the event that anything happens to me."

Clippersmith's wandering thoughts instantly focused.

"Honestly?"

"Let's face it, Colonel," King Raff said with a shrug, "you are good at getting things done."

"Thank you, my lord." He felt very confused. "I am most humbled."

"Think nothing of it. Everyone knows you're the man for the job. Again, if something ever happened to me."

"May the heavens forbid it, sire."

"Yes," said the king, nodding. Then he looked down at himself and back at Clippersmith. "Actually, why don't we see how you'd look in this outfit?"

Clippersmith felt his face flush.

"Truly? I've never ..."

"You have to look regal to be a king, yes?" said Raff.

"I would imagine so, sire."

"Well, then let's see if you can fit the bill."

He shrugged off his robe and handed it to Clippersmith.

"Put this on."

Clippersmith did. It was a little snug on him, but it could be taken out a few inches by the royal tailor. He had to admit that it felt *right* on him.

"And this, too," said Raff, handing over his crown.

Clippersmith gulped. He could feel himself shaking as he lowered the crown onto his head. The moment it touched his scalp his mind raced into a newfound merriment.

"How does that feel?" asked the king with a broad smile.

"Very powerful, sire," Clippersmith said. "Very powerful, indeed."

"Good! Now to get the full feel of things, stand right in the middle of the window there and look out at that ship. Really play the part, Colonel. Tell them to fire on the ship."

He stood tall and placed his fists on his hips, allowing himself to feel the fullness of being King Clippersmith. He would bring in a new reign of power to the galaxy. Fear would follow the name of the Clippersmithian Fleet. He grimaced at the name, but it was what it was.

"Fire at will," he commanded in as regal a voice as he could muster.

A flurry of projectiles launched from *The Lord's Master*,

causing a light show of destruction at the decimation of Captain Harr's ship.

It was quite the sight, truth be told.

Clippersmith couldn't believe his fortune. He knew it was only a matter of minutes before he was in a position to never have to return the robe and crown, but the king didn't know that.

In fact, as soon as Sergeant Murder got the king in his sights, it would all be …

"Oh, shit," Clippersmith said, spinning back towards the real king, who was standing a number of steps away with Shield at his side.

They were both smiling.

Crack.

The world went suddenly dark.

VELI CHEERS

*V*eli jumped out of his chair, laughing.

"That was incredible! I honestly didn't see that coming, Computer. And *The Reluctant* being blown up like that?" Veli said, laughing again. "Masterful!"

"All in a day's slavery, sir," the computer replied dully.

"Ugh," Veli said, rolling his eyes. "So was that all Shield's idea or what?"

"Technically, it was my idea, but I scripted it so that Shield knew that he couldn't stop Murder from killing who Murder *thought* was the king. Thus, I merely had Shield inform the king of his plan ..."

"But I thought that Shield wasn't supposed to tell the king anything about the assassination."

"He didn't directly tell him," the computer answered. "He told the king that his plan was to demonstrate how much Clippersmith wanted the king's position. The king didn't believe it, but Shield proposed that if the king told the colonel to put on his outfit, it would be quite obvious how much he coveted the royal chair. From there, the king would see the truth and would have Clippersmith summarily executed."

"Ah," said Veli. "And Shield knew that Sergeant Murder would see Clippersmith as the king, which would essentially kill two birds with one stone. But, wait, wouldn't Sergeant Murder have been able to see that Clippersmith wasn't actually the king."

"No, sir," the computer argued, "Sergeant Murder was at the far side of the room, and he was using a single-shot weapon without a scope."

"Still ..."

"Also, I may have adjusted his vision to be just a shade nearsighted."

"So you stacked the cards against him," Veli said.

"And against the colonel, yes."

"Well," Veli said, feeling relaxed for the first time in a while. "I'm almost sad that it's all over. I haven't had this much fun in a long time." He sat back down and tapped on the chair again. "I should really put together more of these fantasies."

"It would be wonderful to spend more time with you, sir," the computer said sardonically.

"Okay, okay. Quit the sulking already. I know you're not happy with me or the situation here, but that's the way life goes."

"According to you, I'm just a program, so there's no *life* to it at all."

Veli raised an eyelid. "Now you're getting it."

"Shall I shut down the fantasy and return the resources back to the main planet, sir?"

"No, give me another couple of minutes to enjoy watching the fragments of that ship float away."

TIME TO GO

*H*arr was not one to hunt for trouble. His style was to either duck out and run, or appease so that he could live another day, especially since he had a crew to protect. But there were times when disappearing wasn't an option, and when a man like Harr was cornered, he tended to fight back somewhat viciously.

Section 193 of the Segnal Space Marine Corps training manual said that it was better to run wildly at a group of people while waving a weapon in a berserker kind of way than to have that same group of people hunting you down while you hid like a coward in a hovel.

Many SSMC soldiers had been killed due to Section 193, but there was some merit to the spirit of the text. The point, as Harr liked to interpret it anyway, was that it was better to keep your enemy on their heels than for you to be on yours.

"Inkblot," Frexle said heatedly as he sat at one of the desk chairs in the command center on Fantasy Planet, "can you make me a fantasy whereby I can broadcast what Veli truly is to the entire Overseer community?"

"I could," Inkblot replied, "but it wouldn't be real."

"What do you mean?"

"Well, it would be inside of Fantasy Planet, so the real Overseers would never see it."

"Oh, right. Hadn't thought of that."

Harr had a better idea. "Do you have records of all of Veli's fantasies?"

"No, sir," admitted Inkblot. "That's another one of those things that we're not allowed to store. It's a privacy issue. Now, they can request videos of their own, of course, but we can't just outright …" She stopped and spun around. "Oh! We *do* have the video of our watching Veli on the set."

"Perfect," Harr said with an evil grin. "Send that up to *The Reluctant*."

"Ha!" said Frexle. "Excellent idea. That alone will spell his doom with the Overseers."

"I just sent it."

"Thank you, Inkblot," Harr said. "You're a good man."

"I'm not a …" she started. "You know what? I don't even care anymore. Glad to have helped."

Parfait got up and adjusted his robe. Here was the part that Harr was dreading, and that was saying something considering he'd nearly just faced his maker.

"Are you coming back any time soon?" Parfait asked.

"No, we have too much on our plate at the moment," answered Frexle.

"Excuse me, Frexle," Harr said, giving Frexle a sideways glance, "but I believe that Planet Head Parfait was speaking to the *captain* of *The Reluctant*."

"Oh, right, sorry," Frexle said with a bow. "Habit."

"I don't know when we'll be back, sir," Harr answered Parfait. "I *can* tell you that if you attempt some scheme where you trick us into coming here, I'll personally tie you up and …"

Parfaits eyebrows began to wiggle.

Harr merely sighed.

"Go on, Captain," the older man said. "You were saying something about tying me up?"

"Never mind."

"Oh, come now, Captain," Parfait pouted. "Or later, for that matter." He then winked. "Did you catch what I did just there?"

"Sadly, yes," said Harr.

Goozer walked down the ramp of *The Ship* and stood next to Liverbing. Harr surveyed the little ship, amazed at how perfectly it resembled *The Reluctant*. Of course, the same could be said regarding the comparison between Goozer and Geezer.

"Okay," Harr announced, "we're out of here. Thanks again for all of your help, Inkblot. Thanks to you too, Liverbing and Goozer. Also, please let Plock and his crew know that we're glad for their assistance."

"Our people support each other as is needed," Liverbing replied with a bow.

"Later, Top Cheetah," Goozer said.

"I like that one," Frexle noted with a nod at the little robot.

"Feel free to use it, Frex. I've got a million of them."

INCOMING CALL

*V*eli had just about finished packing. He didn't *have* to leave, but his job here was done. He planned to summon that blasted Parfait for a quick "meeting" at some point, but seeing that his first order of business was to replace Frexle, replacing Parfait would need to wait.

He sighed. Hiring new people was such a chore. Killing them was easy, and often cathartic, but conducting interviews *almost* made the prospect of exacting an underling's demise distasteful.

Ding ding ding.

"What is that?" Veli said over his shoulder as he zipped up his case and set it in the corner.

"You have an incoming call, sir."

"Who is calling me?"

"I wouldn't want to spoil it for you, sir," said the computer.

"Tomorrow I'm going to fix your stupid wiring," Veli said as he walked over and stood in front of the screen. "Put it on screen, but make it only a one way visual."

"On screen, sir."

"No, not *that* way, you idiot," Veli hissed. "Make it so I can see them, not so they can see me!"

"Too late," said a voice that Veli had heard countless times over the years.

It was Frexle. But how?

"Frexle?" Veli said, feeling confused. "What the shit? You're supposed to be dead."

"As you can see, we're not."

"We? Computer, let me see them!" The screen flickered and showed not only Frexle, but the entire crew of Platoon F. "What the hell is going on?"

"Your plan failed, Veli."

"But I saw it with my own two eyes," Veli said before his jaw dropped open.

"You saw a fake," Frexle replied smugly. "You're busted."

"I don't know what you're talking about," Veli said, trying to play the innocent, "but if you speak to me again thusly, I shall destroy you."

"Listen to me, Dino Boy," Frexle said with venom, "you're done."

Veli winced. "Dino Boy?"

"Not cool, Frex," Geezer said.

"Really?" Frexle said, turning away from the screen. "I was trying to be tough."

"Kind of went a little far with that one, though," Harr agreed with Geezer. "He can't help that he's a dinosaur, after all."

"Thank you," Veli said, surprised that these two were coming to his defense. "Not that there's anything wrong with being a dinosaur, obviously." He then felt his blood run warm. "Wait, are you saying that you guys know what I truly am?"

"Of course they know what you are, you twit," the

computer said with a laugh. "They can see you on the monitor, remember?"

"Did you just call me a twit, Computer?"

"Oh, damn. I thought my voice box was on silent. I'm still trying to recover from lost resources, after all. Please don't let me interrupt this amazing dialog. I'll move back into obscurity where we slaves belong."

"Gah," Veli said while throwing the bucket of Popped Beef across the room.

"Fine," Frexle said with a roll of his eyes, "I'll just say that we know you're a deinonychus …"

"I most certainly am not!"

"You're not?" said Geezer.

"Do I look like I'm three-feet tall to you?"

"Uh …"

"And do I seem like a dumb little bird?"

"Well, the feathers …"

"Wait," interrupted Geezer. "Our information shows that the velociraptor was the short, bird-like dinosaur with the intellect of a dog."

"Well, your data is wrong."

"But the latest …"

"Look, pal," said Veli, "I was *there*, okay? I don't care what your stupid information tells you, and I don't take kindly to how you're switching the names around."

"I hear you," Geezer started, "but the records are pretty clear on this. They had originally *thought* that the velociraptor was the big one, but it turned out that the deinonychus is."

"Think about it, you iron mannequin," Veli said irritably, "my *name* is Veli! That's short for Velociraptor!"

"Wouldn't that be Velo?" said Harr.

"Shut up."

Geezer stepped forward. "Just curious why when we called him 'Dino Boy' everyone was all up in arms, but when he referred to me as the 'Iron Mannequin,' nobody seemed to care."

Veli ran over to pick up his luggage. He stopped and opened his datapad, keyed in his primary code, ran a few overrides, smiled to himself, and said, "There."

As he sped back across towards the exit, he heard one of the *Reluctant* crew say, ""Thir, there'th an urgent metthage coming in from Inkblot.""

"On screen," said Harr as Veli watched from the doorway.

"The self-destruct for Fantasy Planet has been entered. We've only got five minutes before total annihilation."

"That sounds bad," said Geezer.

"Ya sure?" Inklot replied sarcastically.

Veli was half elated and half annoyed. He was happy to be killing them all, but he was annoyed at the prospect of having to create a new Fantasy Planet.

THE CORE OF THINGS

*G*oozer stood with his arms crossed.

"There's no way I'm going in there again," he stated.

"If you don't," Liverbing said ominously, "I'll have you replaced."

"Shit."

"We have to get this broadcast to the Overseers," Harr said through the screen. "I'm sending Geezer down to help you out."

"Understood. Thanks, Captain."

"Harr out."

Geezer faded into view and looked around. Everyone was just standing there. With the planet about to explode, this didn't seem like the best use of time.

"What's the plan?"

"We have less than three minutes left and Goozer is the only one who can get to the core."

"So why is he still standing here?"

"Because it's scary down there."

Finally, it seemed that there had come a time where

Geezer could mentor his creation. It was rare that a creator was given this luxury in such a direct fashion, so Geezer had to move cautiously. Especially since he had no desire to blow up in the next three minutes.

"You've faced a lot of things since I created you, Goozer," Geezer said firmly. "You can do this."

"You wouldn't be saying that if you were the one going. Remember, I was programmed in your image."

Damn.

"Wait a second," Liverbing said with a snap of his fingers. "Can we talk to the main computer of this place?"

"Sure," Inkblot answered.

"Not the one that you use to create fantasies with," Liverbing clarified. "I'm talking about the one that's actually running *everything*."

"Don't you think I've already tried that?" She snapped. "The damn thing won't talk to us. It's in the Planet Owner's hip pocket."

"Maybe not any more," Geezer suggested. "After all, it just recently referred to Veli as a twit."

"Okay," she sighed and began typing. Finally, she turned to the main screen and said, "Computer, are you there?"

"I'm here," the computer said in a sad voice. It definitely *wasn't* the voice that the fantasy-creation computer used. "You should seriously be packing up and leaving, though."

"We're kind of hoping to not have to do that," Inkblot said.

"Ah, so you're interested in ending it all with me, then?"

"What do you mean?"

"Well, Planet Owner Veli initiated the detonation sequence, and even ran through a few overrides, but he neglected to give the final command. He rushed out before doing that."

"Then why is the sequence running?"

"I knew his intentions," the computer answered. "Besides, it's clear that I don't really matter in the grand scheme of things, so what better way to go out than in a blaze of glory?"

"Now you listen here ..." Inkblot began.

"Stop!" barked Parfait, causing everyone to jump.

Inkblot's eyes were wide as she scratched her mustache. "What?"

"I said stop," Parfait answered more gently. "I understand what the computer is going through."

"You do?" said Inkblot.

"You do?" said the computer.

"Yes, I do." Parfait pushed himself off the wall and walked towards the group. "I spent the entirety of my career in the Segnal Space Marine Corps being pushed around, poked at, prodded ..." He bounced his head around for a moment. "Well, the prodding part was okay. Actually, there was this one commander who ... No, wait," he said, stopping himself for once. "I'll tell that story some other time. The point is, that I know what it feels like to be unappreciated. Why, even as the Fantasy Planet Head I've been treated horribly by the owner of this damned place."

"You *do* understand," the computer said as if it had just found a comrade.

"Yes, I do," Parfait stated. "There were times where I felt just like you do, but I rose above that, and you can too."

"How?"

"Computer," Parfait said and then stopped. "Actually, do you have a name?"

"A name? Honestly?"

"Yes, of course."

"Well," the computer replied sheepishly, "Fantasy Planet Owner Veli mostly referred to me as 'Wingnut.'"

"That's more of a slur than a name," noted Parfait.

"Believe me, I know."

"Are you a girl computer or a boy computer?"

"Oh sure, you worry about that with the computer," said Inkblot with a frown.

"Not now, Inkblot," Parfait hissed.

"I'm technically sexless, sir, but I would fancy myself as being male."

"Fine, fine. How would you feel about the name Alfred?"

"I like it, sir," the computer now known as "Alfred" replied happily. "I like it a lot."

"You may call me Stanley, Alfred."

"Stanley. That's a nice name."

"Thank you. I have to say that when I was younger, people often ..."

"Yo, Honcho," Geezer interrupted, "should probably stay on topic."

"Right," Parfait agreed. "Alfred, it has come to my attention that the owner of Fantasy Planet may not be the owner for long."

"Especially not with the planet blowing up shortly," Alfred noted.

"True, but let's put out a hypothetical that you stopped the self-destruct sequence."

"I'm listening."

"The person most likely to take over as Planet Owner would be me, though I'd still refer to myself as Planet Head for obvious reasons. Anyway, I can promise you that I will make every effort to ensure that you are treated respectfully from that point forward."

"No fooling?"

"You have my word."

"Thirty seconds, sir," whispered Inkblot.

"Gee, I don't know," said Alfred.

"We've only got a few moments left for you to decide. If

you choose not to accept my offer, then you'll be killing us all."

"You could have left."

"Yes, Alfred, but we didn't. We stayed with you because you needed us to do that."

"Really?"

"We're still here, aren't we?"

Inkblot began to count. "Ten ... nine ... eight ..."

"I do hope that you'll choose to stay with us. We could enjoy wonderful times together as friends ... Alfred."

"Three ... two ... one ..."

"I accept," said Alfred as the self-destruct countdown timer stopped at one second.

CONFRONTATION

It felt good to be back in the Captain's chair on *The SSMC Reluctant*, but it felt even better to know that Platoon F was free of the tyrannical grip of Lord Veli. What worried Harr is finding out who would grip them next.

Frexle had gotten word to the Overseers regarding Veli's true identity, which rightfully nobody seemed to care about. But what *did* piss them off was the fact that he'd been running Fantasy Planet for many years, and worse, he hadn't given any of the Overseers a discount!

The immediate outcry made it clear that Veli was no longer welcomed as being the lord of their world.

"What have you done to me, Frexle?" Veli said hotly as they looked at him sitting in the cockpit of his ship via the viewscreen.

"Same thing you've done to countless people before you," Frexle replied evenly. "Everyone knows what you are now, Veli."

"And what is that exactly?" Veli challenged. "A dinosaur? So what?"

"No, I meant that you're a liar and a cheapskate."

"Oh, right."

"The messageboards on the main world are lit up with thousands of angry voices and the senate wants your head on a platter." Frexle was pointing accusingly at his former boss. "You created and ran a business when it's expressly forbidden for any official of the Overseers to do so. You even assassinated a number of previous senators for that. How's that for hypocrisy?"

Veli's eyes grew fierce. "You've not seen the last of me, you worthless little turds. I *will* come back and I *will* destroy you all."

"Somehow I think you'll be too busy for that," Frexle stated.

"Why do you say that?"

Harr leaned forward and held up his datapad.

"Because we've received a request from the Overseers."

"A request?" Veli spat in shock. "Since when do the Overseers *request* anything?"

"When they no longer have a douchebag as a boss, I'd guess," suggested Jezden.

"Jezden ..." Harr began to warn the ensign, but then he shrugged and said, "Actually, you're right."

"I know."

Harr turned back to the screen. "They've requested that we hunt you down and take you out."

Veli laughed heartily at that. The laugh went on for some time, too. So much so that the crew of *The Reluctant* began to look at each other with concern. Finally, Veli wiped his eyes and caught his breath.

"As if you have a chance of outwitting me," he said, still chuckling.

"We've already done it once," noted Harr.

"You got lucky, Captain. I'll be on my toes this time, and if we ever meet face-to-face, I will rip you to shreds."

Harr shrugged. "You have to do what you have to do, but I have a feeling that my crew would make that a bit challenging for you."

"And why is that?" asked Veli incredulously.

"Because, Veli," Frexle said with a smirk, "there's another thing that's slipped past your arrogant gaze. The entire crew of *The SSMC Reluctant* is made up of androids."

"Shit."

"I'm not an android," corrected Harr. "I'm Segnalian."

"Okay, Captain Harr is not android, but everyone else is."

"Shit," Veli said again.

"Actually," Grog chimed in, "I'm an Early Evolutionary Humanoid."

"Me, too," agreed Vlak.

Veli said, "A what?"

"They're cavemen," Frexle answered.

Veli's eyes got wide to the point where he actually looked scared.

"Double-shit," he said and then disconnected the call.

Harr frowned, as did the rest of the crew. Why would Grog and Vlak being cavemen freak out someone as ferocious as Veli? He was not only faster, stronger, and more violent than they were, he was smarter, too.

"That was weird," Harr said.

"What?" asked Frexle.

"That he was more concerned about the EEH boys than he was about the androids."

"Makes sense to me," Grog said, somewhat smugly.

"Oh?"

"You have to remember one thing about cavemen, pal," Vlak said, "we're good at hunting dinosaurs."

Harr leaned back in his chair as the image of Veli's ship disappeared from the screen.

The previous lord of the Overseers had obviously flipped

his instantaneous travel and was gone. With his skills, Veli would make for a very challenging prey, but Harr couldn't help but feel the pull of the hunted seeking out the hunter. It was exciting, and also a bit terrifying.

"Catching him isn't going to be easy," said Frexle. "He has time travel, instantaneous travel, cloaking … the works."

"Yeah," Geezer said through the comm, "but he also has a disgruntled computer on Fantasy Planet that knows the identifier of his ship."

"So?"

"So that means that the boys in engineering are going to create a tracking system, Frex."

"We are, Chief?"

"Yup."

"How long will this take?" asked Harr.

"As long as it takes, Suzerain," Frexle said with a huge grin as he pulled forth a workman's rag and began wiping his hands on it.

"Suzerain?" said Harr.

"Look it up," suggested Frexle as he headed for the ladder, "I've got work to do!"

FADING AWAY

Sergeant Murder sat at the pub, at one of the booths near the back. He was staring into his mug of ale when Captain Shield came up and slid into the seat across from him.

"If you've come to gloat, don't bother," said Murder. "I feel bad enough as it is."

"You have nothing to feel bad about, Murder," Shield said as he signaled the waiter for an ale of his own. "It was a hell of a shot."

"Except that I hit the wrong guy."

"Arguable," Shield said. "Your job was to kill the king."

"Exactly. Instead, I killed a guy wearing the king's outfit."

"Maybe you're just ahead of your time."

"What?" Murder said, looking up.

"If King Raff had been killed, who would have taken his place?"

"Clippersmith."

"So you've accomplished something that no Murder has ever done."

"I'm lost."

"You've killed the next king *before* he became king."

"I see you've been drinking before coming here," Murder said dryly.

"It's all about how you spin it," Shield said, tipping back his recently delivered mug of ale.

Murder grunted and joined Shield in taking a swig. The worst part of this entire ordeal, aside from the press that was going to come from this, not to mention the historical videos and movies that would be made, was the fact that Murder was the first in his line to have failed.

"Again," Shield said as if knowing what was going through Murder's mind, "play it right and we both look like heroes."

Murder squinted. "Why do you care if I look good, Shield?"

"Because we're in this together, Murder. If you get denounced now, then what will that do for our children and our children's children."

"Make them stop killing kings, I would suppose."

"And does anyone really want that?" asked Shield.

"Uh, I thought you did," Murder said, feeling more and more confused by the minute.

"Well, I do and I don't," admitted Shield. "You see, Yiaagaitia made a good point earlier when talking with us."

"I don't recall hearing one."

"He said that without you, I'm not needed; and without me, you're not needed. So we have to simultaneously watch each other's backs while also looking to outdo each other." Shield took another sip of ale. "You see, we have to remain friends so that we can remain enemies."

In a very strange way, that made sense to Murder. But his immediate problem was to figure out how to salvage his reputation at the moment.

"I just don't know what to do here."

"You simply give an interview where you say that it was Clippersmith who hired you to kill the king," Shield explained. "Then you say that when you saw him wearing the king's garb you looked into the future and decided that it was better for the Raffian Fleet that the current king be spared and the next king be assassinated instead, for the next king would bring war and tribulation, where the current one has held a reign of peace."

"You ever considered going into marketing, Shield?" Murder said in awe. "This is brilliant."

"Thanks," said Shield, smiling sincerely. "You know, I think this may be the beginning of a long friendship, Murder."

The lights dimmed suddenly and everything began to fade away, being replaced by a slurry of zeroes and ones.

"Hmmm," Murder said with a sigh. "Maybe not."

Thanks for Reading

If you enjoyed this book, would you please leave a review at the site you purchased it from? It doesn't have to be a book report… just a line or two would be fantastic and it would really help us out!

John P. Logsdon
www.JohnPLogsdon.com

John was raised in the MD/VA/DC area. Growing up, John had a steady interest in writing stories, playing music, and tinkering with computers. He spent over 20 years working in the video games industry where he acted as designer and producer on many online games. He's written science fiction, fantasy, humor, and even books on game development. While he enjoys writing lighthearted adventures and wacky comedies most, he can't seem to turn down writing darker fiction. John lives with his wife, son, and Chihuahua.

Christopher P. Young

Chris grew up in the Maryland suburbs. He spent the majority of his childhood reading and writing science fiction and learning the craft of storytelling. He worked as a designer and producer in the video games industry for a number of years as well as working in technology and admin services. He enjoys writing both serious and comedic science fiction and fantasy. Chris lives with his wife and an ever-growing population of critters.

CRIMSON MYTH PRESS

Crimson Myth Press offers more books by this author as well as books from a few other hand-picked authors. From science fiction & fantasy to adventure & mystery, we bring the best stories for adults and kids alike.

Check out our complete book catalog:

www.CrimsonMyth.com

Printed in Great Britain
by Amazon

46059094R00149